Salvation No Kissing Required

Christina Rowell

Featherweight Press
www.featherweightpublishing.com

This book is a work of fiction. Names, characters, places, and incidents either are products of the author's imagination or are used fictitiously. Any resemblance to actual events or locales or persons, living or dead, is entirely coincidental.

Published by
Featherweight Publishing
3052 Gaines Waterport Rd.
Albion, NY 14411

Visit Featherweight Publishing on the Internet:
www.featherweightpublishing.com

Cover Art by Deana Jamroz
Editing by Kelly Anderson

Print format ISBN# 978-1-60820-856-2
ebook formats also available

Issued 2013

Prologue

Arizona, six months earlier

What's happening? How did this all spiral out of control? The sixteen-year-old boy is confused. With the promises of no rules to obey, eternal life, and sex anytime he wants, with anyone he so desires; yeah, who wouldn't be tempted? Besides, no money need change hands.

However, payment was expected; of course, there was a charge for Utopia. Deep down, he had known it was all too good to be true. The price was non-negotiable, no haggling, no cutting a better deal was possible. What he had been asked for in exchange was priceless, and he just wasn't prepared for it. No, selling his soul to the Devil wasn't something he would ever be prepared for and something he wasn't going to do.

Therefore, he was now fleeing for his life, he needed to get away from Wingate and fast. Luckily, for him, the road was quiet. He had been driving for about an hour, he had only seen one other vehicle in that time and it was following close behind. It had joined the road about three miles back; the driver had not attempted to overtake and was unlikely to do so now, due to the byroad's narrowness. At first he had thought it was a police car following. Somehow, they may have been alerted that he had stolen his father's car, but eventually he had decided it was unlikely his father would notice it was gone before morning.

The tailgating car suddenly closes the distance between them and it's headlights illuminate the rear-view mirror of the boy's vehicle; blinding him on every turn and twist of the winding road. He presses his foot down, hard onto the gas pedal, but the car's response is sluggish. The young driver is certain that the engine is protesting at being pushed so hard.

The two cars reach the summit of the climbing road and the fearful teenager knows that the ground drops steeply down away from the side. He can't see the bottom of the ravine, it's as though it's lurking in the bowels of the earth.

"What the?" the teenage boy yells with surprise, as the pursuing car gently nudges the rear bumper of his. He moves forward slightly in his seat, but his seat belt clicks and saves him from being hurt in any way. His foot is flat to the floor, but his vehicle continues to struggle to pull away from its pursuer. The boy grips the steering wheel as though he's on a white-knuckle ride at the fairground. The road widens around the last bend and will start to drop downhill, towards Highway 87. He hopes the maniac following him will pass then.

Both cars are now traveling at high speed and the awkward curves of the road are hard to negotiate. The inexperienced driver is finding the steering heavy and he knows he is being pulled closer and closer to the edge of the precipice. He's finally approaching the last bend; he glances in his rear-view, but what he sees causes him to lose his concentration. Just for a moment, but a moment too long. The car leaves the road on the bend and the darkness swallows the teenager up like a whale consuming a minnow.

The tailing car doesn't stop; it drives on, no looking back.

Chapter One

Limbo

My name's Dan Pierce; whether or not that's my birth name, I don't really know. You're asking; why don't I know my identity? Good question. But there's also a good answer; I'm Dea...d, and my earthbound memories have been totally wiped out. I'm finding the D word kind of hard to say, so excuse me. That revelation shocked you, didn't it? Well it came as quite a blow to me. In fact, it's a bit of a bummer, when you wake up and realize you're now a spiritual being.

I've discovered that entry into heaven is no mean feat. It's like starting a new college, or university, the powers that be want to make sure that you're qualified for the tasks ahead. When you reach the pearly gates they don't say, "Hey you're dead, come on in."

Firstly, your name's got to be checked against God's database. It used to be called the Book of Life; well it still is, but it's no longer etched on tablets of stone, or written on papyrus. No way, Heaven has invested in a high tech computer system and the gatekeeper accesses the information via an android tablet. I couldn't believe it; the miracles of modern science will never cease to amaze.

Back to the Book of Life, it's literally a journal of your existence. You know, birth name, where you were born, achievements, disappointments, the good and the bad things you did; of course, it helps if you've led a blemish free life and I don't mean a life without zits. Finally, it states where, when, and how you died. Now this data allows God and his trusted elders to judge as to whether you're celestial material.

When I arrived several days ago, or was it several

years ago? Time isn't measured the same way here. Sorry I'm rambling, put it down to shock. I don't even know if it's relevant as to when I arrived, what is relevant to me is the fact that I didn't actually know my name, never mind how I died. But seemingly, this isn't so uncommon.

However, there was a complication in my case and that was the gatekeeper didn't know my details either and he certainly wasn't expecting me. He had no note of my arrival, nada. To cut a long story short, I didn't get in. I was named Daniel Pierce, for the sake of the records and whisked away to Limbo, tout de suite.

That's when I got the devastating news; take a deep breath because this is a shocker. I was told that if they couldn't establish who I was, or why I was there, I'd be thrown into the Lake of Fire for a second death. Well knock me down with a feather, if it wasn't bad enough that I'd died already, I was to die again. No right to appeal, no chance of a reprieve.

Well that was until Mikey, sorry, I mean Archangel Michael, arrived in Limbo yesterday, to speak to me and a bunch of undesirables. He explained that there was a chance of salvation, all was not lost, we could prove that we were worth saving.

He proposed that we enlist in God's army to help defeat the Red Rider, aka Satan and his foot soldiers who are attempting to flex their muscles on Earth. It seems that Satan has escaped from the burning sulfur lake and he is determined to seek revenge on God for the years he has lived in torment. He is proving to be elusive, his army is growing stronger every day, and Heaven needs all the help it can get.

Duh, now who would say no to this opportunity of redemption? Surprisingly enough, some of my fellow suspected hoods did decline. They didn't fancy doing good deeds, obeying God's word, or Devil slaying. But I said, "Bring it on."

Sooo, that's where I'm at in my celestial career. By the way, I'm now an angelet, which is another name for a probationary angel. How long will my internship last? Well how long is a piece of string?

Guys, I'm about to embark on an important journey and I could do with good friends like you around. What I'm saying is, I'd like you to tag along. I'll need someone to sound off to. How about it? I believe I'll be boarding a bus in Las Vegas tomorrow, headed for Phoenix. I hope to see you then.

Chapter Two

"These in white robes - who are they, and where did they come from?"

Revelation 7:13

Phoenix, Arizona

Thanks for deciding to join me. I'll fill you in and then you can keep up with me the rest of the way. I'm sitting near the back of a Greyhound bus, I boarded some seven hours or so ago. Mikey and I arrived on Earth together; he said he had some business to take care of in Las Vegas.

He's most probably following up a sighting of Satan. But from what I can gather, these sightings are as regular as people saying they saw a dead rock 'n' roll star working behind the counter of a burger joint. Scary.

Everything for my mission has been taken care of. I've got clothes, money in my pocket, and even a tablet with an app especially installed for heavenly beings. This app allows Heaven to contact me 24/7 and they can feed me useful information about my assignment, amongst other things.

I also have a small gold stud in my right ear, but it's no normal piece of jewelry, it's a demon early warning device. But it's a prototype, so they're still uncertain on its reliability. That's the boooring stuff out of the way, let's talk about the exciting stuff, like me.

My human form is that of a seventeen-year-old male. I'm not too shy to say that I'm a gooorgeous guy. Amigas, you'll love me. You'll love my buzz cut, my piercing blue eyes, and of course my toned pecks and abs. I'm not quite as tall as I would have liked, but hey, none of us are perfect. Oh, I forgot to say, I'm a little tiger; grrr. Amigos, don't worry, you'll like me a lot too. Why? Because I'm a real cool dude to hang around with, that's why. Need I say more?

I'm feeling pretty exhausted, I've got roughly an hour to go before I reach my destination and meet my guardian, she's called Sylvia Angell. I'll be living with her for now. The cover story is that she's my Aunt and I'm living with her because my parents are working overseas.

With me? Good. I've got a little homework to do, you can read along with me, but not aloud, because I need to concentrate. Information is downloaded in story form on to my tablet, kind of like an e-book, and you'll be able to read what's available to me. No pictures though, so I hope you can read. Duh, that was a stupid thing for me to say, of course you can!

Hopefully no little gremlins, or devils as the case may be, manage to hack into my system and tamper with my data. The IT department is working on security software as we speak. Unfortunately for heaven, they have no software available here as yet to secure their system.

Oh and another thing, if you see quotes from the bible dotted here and there, well these are little messages sent to me by the Elders. They have a couple of purposes, some are for my spiritual guidance, you know; so I remember that I'm on God's side and he's on mine. The others give me an indication, or as I like to call it; step for a hint, as to what my day ahead may be all about.

The step for hint stuff is based on information gathered from Earth. I suppose it's what government agencies would call their intelligence. Now I have no idea if this intelligence is gathered from intelligencers, a bug in Satan's chambers, or geek angels analyzing incoming data.

All I know is that I have to take some direction from

these messages and act upon them where appropriate. With me so far? Good. Right, eyes down, get reading.

§ § §

Paul's Story

"Now Paul, you take care walking home. Don't detour, and use your cell phone to call your pop at the first sign of trouble." The small, gray haired woman is full of concern and apprehension as she addresses her grandson.

"Gran, stop fussing. I'm a big boy now." The six foot, one hundred and seventy pound seventeen-year-old tries to make light of her anxiety.

"I know you are, but it's not like it was when I was a teenager. You could safely walk for miles and not a soul would bother you."

"Gran, nothing's like it was when you were a teenager. You're prehistoric."

The old woman slaps the young man playfully across the back of the hand. Then throwing her arms around him, she hugs him with all her might.

"Goodbye, I'll call you later," says the teenager and he kisses his Gran on her cheek.

"Goodbye, I love you Paul."

"I love you too Gran." The young man leaves his grandmother standing on the top step of her front porch. He stops before finally stepping onto the sidewalk. He turns around, blows her a kiss, and then goes on his way. She blows one back and she continues to wave until he is out of sight.

It isn't just Paul Mitchum's grandmother who's apprehensive about her grandson's walk home, Paul has his own doubts. But his father made it clear in their last man-to-man talk that he expected his son to fight his own battles. He told him that "he needed to start acting like a man."

When his father, George, went off on one, as he regularly

did since Paul's mom had gone, there was no reasoning with him. There were regular heated exchanges of words between father and son, caused by George drinking copious amounts of liquor.

On these occasions, Paul is left with no alternative but to lock himself away in his bedroom. Only coming out when he hears his pop snore, after him falling into a deep alcohol fueled sleep. Paul's only confidante is his Gran, but he doesn't like to tell her about his rows with his pop. After all it seemed disrespectful, speaking to her about her own son.

§ § §

Phoenix, Bus Depot

My bus draws into the depot, and I'm feeling slightly nervous about the challenges that lie ahead. There is only one man waiting, as the bus finally draws to a halt. I know this has to be Aunt Sylvia's neighbor Isais. I stand up and tug at my backpack; it drops heavily from the overhead parcel shelf onto my seat.

Making my way down to the front exit, I notice the deep-set eyes of the waiting man scour the length of the bus, presumably in search of me. He hasn't caught sight of me yet. I start to descend the steps of the bus, and now he's looking straight at me.

"Are you Sylvie's ward, Daniel?" His Native American face lights up, he sure is a good-looking man for an oldie. I mean to say he's over forty years old.

"I am, but call me Dan. You must be Isais Bia?"

"I surely am boy and you can call me Isais." He chuckles at what he thinks is a witty reply and continues, "Sylvie will be so glad you've arrived safely. She's been baking pies all day. She's even tackled a new 'un, mango and banana. Hell knows what that'll taste like." He slaps me on the back heartily. Putting his large arm around my shoulders, he pulls me towards him and hugs me.

My internal organs feel as though they have just been squished like an accordion.

According to my app, he's six feet five inches and two hundred and seventy pounds. His large frame dwarfs all of my five feet seven inches, one hundred and thirty seven pounds. I can't help but like this guy, I hope we're going to be very good friends.

"Isais, I don't care what the pie tastes like, I'm starved."

"Boy, you sure could do with some of Sylvie's pies inside you. Fatten you up a bit. Give me your backpack; it looks as though the weight of it is going to snap you in two." His arm remains tight around my shoulders and I gladly hand over my bag.

His firm grip assures me that I'm in safe hands. As he guides me through the large bus depot, my feet only make contact with the ground on every second or third step I take. I must look like a puppet or cartoon character.

Finally we're out into the warm July night, the parking bays across from the depot are all taken. I couldn't even take a guess at what this guy's going to drive. Whatever it is, it's going to have to be big.

"That's my truck over there." Isais releases his grip on me. His big long legs take such wide strides that I have no alternative but to start running. We cross the street to an old battered Nissan, Isais puts a key into the driver's door, and the central locking clicks. "Climb in boy, I'll throw your bag in the back." Isais opens the rear passenger door and I hear my bag thump onto the seat.

I climb up into the front passenger side and look around. Brightly colored throws cover the leather seats of the truck and a small leather bound dream catcher hangs from the rear-view mirror. Its blue colored beads catch the street light and its feathers move with a wisp from the warm breeze that's coming in through the now open driver's door. There's a picture of a kid around my age fixed to the dashboard. I wonder if Isais has a son. I wasn't told about one, but then again maybe it's for me to find out.

Isais climbs in, the truck groans gently under his weighty movement, then he starts the engine and we move out into the flow of traffic and head North.

"How long will it take us to reach Aunt Sylvia's, Isais?"

"Twenty minutes ride to Wingate, boy," says Isais cheerfully.

"How long have you been a neighbor of Aunt Sylvia's, or Sylvie as you call her?"

"Sylvie is my pet name for her. How long? Eh, I'm not sure exactly how long, because it seems as though I've known her forever." Isais scratches his head, as if in a hope that he's going to come up with the answer to my question. But I think that's one question he isn't going to be able to answer.

§ § §

Isais and I continued to chat non-stop, like long lost friends, for the journey. The kid in the picture is his son. But it seems I won't have the pleasure of meeting him. The kid's the D word, same as me. I felt like such an idiot when I asked about him, but hey ho, I had to ask. We finally turn into a small street located in what I am reliably informed is the older side of town. The wide streets is lined with small single story homes; cacti and palms fill the gardens.

The truck stops in front of number six, North Orange, Wingate, Scottsdale. The porch lights are on and a woman I can only assume is my new aunt sits on a rocking chair. As I jump out of the truck, she smiles and outstretches her arms. I think I'm going to like her.

Chapter Three

"Lord, help me!"

Matthew 15:25

Paul's Story

Paul knew if he was going to come face to face with his adversaries it would be around the next corner. Paul's breathing is shallow, he's overwhelmed with fear. Beads of sweat form on his forehead and top lip. He walks at a steady pace, treating every noise he hears with suspicion.

"Meow, meow, meo…ow." A screeching black cat darts behind him and leaps over a garden fence and vanishes from sight. Paul is so startled that his heart is now thumping; every beat reverberates through his body. He turns right after Henry's Pharmacy, the street is quiet. He decides to quicken his pace, around the next corner will be East Orange and he'll be on the home run.

"You're out late tonight nerd," a voice speaks from the cover of the shadows. A voice that Paul instantly recognizes. Two young men step out from behind a parked pick-up and stop the young man in his tracks.

"Kurt, I don't want any trouble." Paul takes a sharp intake of breath when he catches sight of the stiletto Kurt's holding.

"Trouble. Why would there be any trouble between you an' me nerd?" Kurt Hills scrapes the edge of the blade frighteningly along Paul's chin. Both he and his lackey, Robbie Dillon, are smaller in stature than Paul, but unlike them, he never carries a weapon. Paul tries to walk on, but Robbie quickly stamps on his foot with force, causing the fearful young man to stagger into Kurt.

"Why are you pushing me out of the way nerd? If I wasn't a forgivin' kind of guy, I'd think you were trying to start some

kind of a fight." Kurt pushes Paul with force, turns towards his friend and says to him, "Aren't I a forgivin' kind of guy, Robbie?"

"You are, Kurt, you are." Robbie smirks.

"I ne, ne..., never pushed you deliberately Kurt. It was an accident. I must have lost my footing." Paul is scared, he's unsure of what to do.

"Do you hear that Robbie? The nerd lost his footing." Kurt laughs sinisterly.

"A bit clumsy if you ask me, Kurt." Robbie forces a laugh. Kurt takes a step forward and walks straight into Paul, using his full body weight as he does so. Paul loses his balance and falls backwards onto the parked car his two attackers had previously hidden behind. His back slams down onto the hard metal, winding him momentarily.

In the event that Paul might fight back, Robbie takes no chances and kicks Paul's legs away from him, leaving the young victim lying over the hood. Gravity takes over and Paul thuds to the ground. Kurt sneers and kicks Paul hard in the gut, causing Paul to coil in pain. A laughing Robbie is eager to inflict further harm and poises his foot over a prostrated Paul's head.

Dread fills Paul in anticipation of Robbie's foot making contact with him. He tries to shield his face from the foot he can see coming towards him. He feels as if everything is taking place in slow motion. He takes a deep breath, to ready his body for the pain, then, beep, beep, beep. The vehicle's horn sounds loudly and its lights begin flashing intermittently. The unexpected bursts of orange lights illuminate the victim's anguish.

"Get away from my truck, you little... Get away, I've called 911," a man's voice shouts angrily from one of the nearby houses.

The aggressors scatter into opposite directions, leaving Paul on the ground like a great oak that has just been felled.

Paul picks himself up with some urgency, as he can hear a police siren in the distance. His body aches but he wants to make himself scarce before the police arrive. There would be too many questions in need of answers.

He hurries the short distance before turning the corner into the relative safety of East Orange. He was home, battered and bruised, but home.

§ § §

Aunt Sylvia's pies are lying in a line along the pine kitchen counter. The room is large and a round table covered in a floral cloth dominates the room. The smell of home baking and freshly ground coffee makes Sylvia's house into a home. I settle down at the table just as Isais returns from taking my backpack into my new bedroom.

"I've put Daniel's things in the back room Sylvie, is that okay?" Isais looks for approval from Sylvia, but she's so absorbed in cutting her pies that she doesn't reply to him. He raises his eyebrows and smiles. Seemingly unaware that she's been spoken to, Aunt Sylvia is now carefully placing an assortment of slices onto each of the three plates in front of her, with a thick dollop of whipped cream on the side. Her concentration is only broken when the contents of the coffee pot starts to hiss and spit as it bubbles over onto the stove.

"Oh my goodness. Yes, that's fine Isais. I'm sorry I ignored you just now. Please do me another favor Isais; pour the coffee that's spilling all over my stove into the cups on the table." She jumps each time the discharging liquid lands on the hot metal rings and makes a sizzling noise.

"Sure will." Isais gets up from the table and goes over to the stove. He places a folded dishcloth in his hand, to make sure he doesn't get burnt, before lifting the hot, bubbling pot off the stove. It stops spurting instantly.

"Can I do anything Aunt Sylvia?" I know I'm a bit

late in offering to help, but maybe I should do something other than drool.

"The only thing you need to do right now, Daniel, is give me your verdict on my pies." With an overflowing plate in each hand, Aunt Sylvia walks over to the table. Putting one of them down in front of me, she says, "Now eat boy, eat."

She watches me with anticipation as I lift up my fork and cut one of the slices into more manageable, bite size pieces. Her eyes never leave my face as I put the first forkful into my mouth and chew.

"Awesome, Aunt Sylvia. Awesome." The flavor of mango and banana explodes in my mouth. She tousles my hair, well, what hair I have left since Mikey ordered a barber to take the clippers over my head in Las Vegas. I think I have a look of a famous R & B star, especially when I wear my fedora. You'll just need to use a little imagination. In fact, as you can't see me, you can imagine I look like anyone you want me to, in your mind's eye. Sorry, I digress.

"Plenty more to go round, boys. What do you think of my mango and banana pie then, Isais?" Aunt Sylvia sits down in the chair next to me; she's now watching Isais tuck into his plate of pie. Each large man bite he takes is followed by a slurp of coffee, much to her amusement.

"Awesome, Sylvie. Awesome." Isais sprays Aunt Sylvia and me with crumbs from his mouth as he tries to mimic me. We all erupt with laughter. All I can say is, he better not give up the day job, as he'll never make it big as an impressionist.

Chapter Four

Remember not the sins of my youth.

Psalm 25:7

Jenny's Story

Jenny Green is lying on top of her bed staring into space when her cell phone starts to ring. On the display screen she can see it's her boyfriend calling.

"Hi Kurt, I'm sorry I don't think I can see you tonight." She had been dreading this call.

"What do you mean you don't think you can see me tonight?" says Kurt angrily. When he says jump, he expects others to say 'how high?', and his girlfriend is no exception. "I see you every night. I'll see you, usual place, or are you meeting some other guy?" He isn't going to accept excuses.

"No. Of course not. I love you Ku..." Jenny can feel the tears prick her eyes as Kurt hangs up. Why did he constantly get so mad with her? They made out most nights, even when she didn't want to.

She had just wanted to explain that her mother had suggested that they should spend some quality time together. The suggestion came out of the blue and it was unlikely to happen again in a long while.

Jenny's mother, Gabriella, is a forty-something, going on twenty, divorcee. She goes clubbing with her friends most nights, meaning that Jenny can normally do as she pleases, with no questions asked. The young woman is treating her mother's newfound caring side with mistrust. But as she's always longed to have a close relationship with her mother, like other girls at school have, she's willing to give it a go.

But what is she going to do about Kurt? She doesn't want to do anything that might cause her to lose him. She is the envy of all the girls at school, as he's Wingate High's promising sports star of the future. Her mind drifts, she dreams of them together in the years to come, she'll have fancy clothes and jewelry and they'll guest at red carpet events. Kurt promises her it all.

There's a knock at Jenny's bedroom door. "Jenny, the pizzas are here. I've put your favorite chick flick in the DVD player. Cold beer for me, cold soda for you. We're all set." Gabriella enters the room. Jenny doesn't reply, her mind is racing. She can't let Kurt down, he can get any other girl he wants. "Okay a cold beer for you as well. One won't do you any harm." Gabriella tries to coax a response from her daughter.

"I don't want pizza. I don't want beer. In fact I don't want you," shouts Jenny defensively at her mother and she suppresses her tears of frustration.

"You ungrateful little tramp. I could have been out with Andy tonight." Gabriella is angry at her daughter's outburst.

"Don't let me spoil your night," screams Jenny.

"Spoil my night. You've spoiled my life. Don't bother coming down for pizza." As she storms out of her daughter's bedroom, Gabriella slams the door closed behind her.

"Bitch," shouts Jenny after her mother. Glaring at the closed wooden door, she wishes that she could see through it. She wants her mother to know how much she hates her. After all, her mother has just made it very clear that she has no love for her at all. Gabriella's beloved little dog, Kushi, has always been at the forefront of her mother's affections. "Bitch."

§ § §

"Goodnight Isais. Thanks for the lift and the company. Probably see you tomorrow." I walk with Isais to the front door.

"Probably will. Goodnight boy, enjoy school." He gives me one of his now familiar big hugs. As I close the door, I can hear Isais laugh loudly as he makes his way down the front path.

I walk into the kitchen where Aunt Sylvia is putting away the dishes that Isais and I washed and dried earlier.

"Daniel, sit down at the table, we need to have a little chat. I'll be with you in a moment." I instantly realize by Aunt Sylvia's tone that she takes the role of guardian very seriously. Now that we're alone we'll be able to get to know each other a bit better.

"Sure, time to get down to business." My bravado is to cover up the fact that I'm now feeling rather nervous. Although the word nervous is an understatement; I'm totally petrified. Whilst Isais was with us, the evening had been happy and relaxed. But I knew the serious stuff would have to be raised at some point in the evening.

"Daniel, do you understand why you are here with me?"

"Yes. Mikey explained, sorry I mean Archangel Michael." I don't mean to be discourteous towards her or Mikey. I hope she's okay with what I just said. Things are good, she's smiling.

"I'm sure it was all explained to you, but I'd like to reiterate a very important point; you're here because you need to prove that you deserve salvation." Her voice is so gentle, kind of hypnotic. I'm not sure if she wants me to say anything or not. If in doubt, which I am, I think I'd better wait for her to speak again. Phew, she's opening her mouth. "You'll be tested on various things. We angels require a multitude of strings to our harps. We offer everyday guidance, healing, support, as well as spiritual guidance. We also need to demonstrate that we can protect, deliver others and ourselves from evil. Unfortunately for Earth, Satan is at large and more humans than normal need our help right now." Her eyes search my face. I think she's probably weighing me up.

"Seems simple enough." I'm trying to sound confident,

but I'm quaking in my boots. Aunt Sylvia seems to find my statement as amusing as you probably did; she titters in an angel like manner. Not that you would know how an angel titters and I have no time to mimic her titter at present. I have a few things that I want to clear up and now would probably be as good a time as any to get my questions out of the way.

"I've had two kid's profiles downloaded to me, but no pictures, how will I know them?" This has been quite a puzzle to me.

"The information you have been provided with is pretty accurate. For one, you have their names and a few discreet inquiries around school should point you in their direction."

"Okay I never thought of that. That's put my mind a bit more at ease about the good guys. What about the bad ones?" I only asked the question because I thought you would want to know.

"Unlike the good guys, as you like to call them, you won't always know them. The Devil and his accomplices come in all shapes and disguises. They will endeavor to seduce you and enlist you in their wicked, cruel ways. Going with the Red Rider will do nothing but lead to your ruin and your heavenly ambitions will be destroyed." No smiles from her this time.

"I can understand why you chuckled earlier. If my enemies aren't easily identified, things are going to be a little more difficult than I first anticipated. In fact, I was being cocky."

"I don't think you were being cocky; you were being a tad naive. I know this is something that you will have been told already, but there is no harm in me going over it again. You do have a slight advantage over the Devil's new recruits. The power of good, given to you by our Lord, will help protect you from their attacks. But once their souls have been fully possessed by the Red Rider, I'm afraid it will be a matter of good versus evil. And we can only pray that the good you have been empowered with will win. Now, do you have any other questions?" Aunt Sylvia is a real sensitive lady. The only problem I can see with the powers I've been given is that no one has actually explained what they are. Mikey told me that it's all about gaining hands-on experience.

"Do you think I'll ever have any recollection of who I am, how I died, or will heaven even be able to establish the true facts?" I'm starting to feel rather anxious about this whole thing, especially the devil slaying part. Maybe I should have jumped in the lake, saved them the trouble.

"Your memory should gradually return. I will try and explain what's happening the best way I can. Following accidents, trauma, and bad experiences, some humans suffer from amnesia. They can't recall past memories, or retain current happenings until their brain deals with what caused it to forget in the first place.

"In the same way, you're having to come to terms with the traumatic experience of death. This in turn, has caused your recollection process to go into lock down. Dan, don't build your hopes up, it may take some time. In fact, it could take years before you will remember anything about yourself. Of course there is also the risk that when you do recollect, you'll wish you never had."

"Do you think Heaven will find out my true identity in the near future?"

"Dan, these are very unusual circumstances. The Gatekeeper keeps excellent records and you're proving to be an enigma."

"Mmm. Let's hope I'm a good guy then."

"Dan, even if you're not, I am on your side and I will help you when and where I can. As will the other celestial beings who watch over you. This is your big chance, grab it with both hands."

Something that will surprise you is I'm kind of lost for words. I look at Sylvia for some kind of assurance.

"Now when you go to bed think hard about what I've said to you. Now let us pray."

She smiles and takes my hand.

If it was possible for me to run for the door and head for the hills, I would do it right now, at this minute. But somehow I think the celestial beings would find me. I better just pray and hope that someone up there is listening to the pleading in my voice. We both say in unison,

"Our Father who art in heaven..."

Chapter Five

For wisdom will enter your heart, and knowledge will be pleasant to your soul.

Discretion will protect you, and understanding will guard you.

Proverbs 2:10, 11

Wingate High School

I don't know if I should be scared about the schooling side of things, because I do seem to be quite an intelligent guy. The test results I have with me verify that. But whose actual test results are they? It's funny, although I can't remember anything about my past life, the things I'm expected to know just seem to pop into my head. So let's hope, and of course pray, that I'll know the answers in my English and math classes.

I arrived early for my appointment at the school registration office. I've been sitting here in the reception area for a good twenty minutes. It's now 7:45 a.m. and that's the time I'm suppose to meet up with a counselor, Adriana Moffat, to go over my paperwork.

Classes already started at 7:30 a.m. so I'm late for the first one. I can see a large, round shaped, stern looking woman walking towards me from the other side of the open plan office.

"You must be Daniel." She has a really loud voice.

"Yes." I stand up and walk towards her.

"Well Daniel, I'm Ms. Moffat. If you follow me over to my desk we'll finalize your registration." She gives me a big smile. Heck, she's not so stern after all. Thank you Lord. I follow her to her desk and we both sit down. She looks at the monitor of her computer, then at me and she says, "Daniel, I hope you have all the correct documents with you today." She looks back at the monitor and depresses a couple of keys on the keyboard in front of her.

"I hope so too." I pull open the plastic wallet I've been nursing for the last half hour and I remove the contents. I push the papers across the desk towards her and I say, "I've brought my immunization certificate, birth certificate, my academic test results, and custody papers showing my Aunt Sylvia is my guardian angel."

"Guardian angel?" Ms. Moffat is looking at me quizzically. I can't believe I just said guardian angel. I slipped up there. I'm going to have to think on my feet.

"That's my pet name for Aunt Sylvia. With her surname being Angell and her, eh, being my legal guardian. It's a little joke we have going on. Probably not as funny as we think it is." I laugh nervously. Does what I've just said count as a lie? The room doesn't erupt into flames, so hopefully no sin was committed.

"Oh yes, that's nice." Ms. Moffat gives me a big empathetic smile. She taps her large fingers on the keyboard of her PC once more. I assume she's locating more of my records. Her eyes move across the screen rapidly, reading the information in front of her. She looks back down at my paperwork and starts to flick through it. She shakes her head, looks back at the screen, then starts to thumb through the documents again. "Oh dear Daniel, when I met with your aunt I told her that I needed some proof of address from her. You know, a utility bill or mortgage payments, something like that. I've got all the personal paperwork I need from you. But I need that from your aunt before I can complete registration and let you go to class. This means you can't start class today."

I feel a bit disappointed that things aren't going according to plan. But I believe there must be a reason for this little hiccup. Maybe the lie did count as a sin. I take a deep breath; I need to prepare myself for the worst. Okay, perhaps I am dramatizing this whole hell and damnation thing. In fact, I'm milking it.

This has just been an oversight. I wonder if there is something I can say, or do, that will make Ms. Moffat take pity on me. Trying to adopt an air of sadness, I drop my head. If you could see me, I'm now displaying the best ever sad look. But there's no need, because abracadabra, and there's no hocus-pocus that I know of, I've just left some of the papers in the folder. Duh, must be my nerves.

"Ms. Moffat, I must have overlooked this when I handed my documents over." I don't read the piece of paper I'm handing over; I'm just crossing my fingers it's what she wants.

"Excellent Daniel." My counselor looks over at what I guess is a utility bill of some sort and then she gives me a broad smile. "Daniel, welcome to Wingate High School, the school for winners. Now here's your timetable and information on the school. It includes a map of the campus. On top I've placed the school's mission and vision statements. If you give me five minutes, I'll take you along to your first class, which is math. If you could go sit in reception for now."

I give a little sigh of relief. God does work in mysterious ways.

§ § §

Ten minutes have passed and I'm still in the waiting area, twiddling my thumbs. Hey, I can pass the time by reading the Mission Statement. Do you want to read it with me? Sorry, you've no choice.

The mission of Wingate High School's students is that,

They aim to be **<u>W</u>**inners in life.

Their **I**ntegrity is their being united as one whole.

They are **N**oble and deserve the admiration that may be bestowed upon them.

They are **G**ifted academics and athletes.

They are **A**chievers and successfully do it, or cause it to happen.

They are **T**olerant and allow others to have their own attitudes or beliefs, even if they do not agree, or approve.

They **E**xcel in everything they do.

I like this statement. However, I've no time to chatter, because I can see Ms. Moffat coming towards me. It's time to go into the real world.

§ § §

Paul's Story

George Mitchum had been lying in a drunken stupor when Paul had arrived home the previous night and he was still in bed when Paul had left for school this morning. Paul was glad his father hadn't been around first thing, because he would have demanded some answers about his son's visible injuries.

Following his fracas with Kurt and Robbie, Paul's cheekbone is scraped and swollen, as well as his face being slightly black and blue. But his facial injuries are minor compared to the bruising he has on his torso. He also has a severe pain in his rib area, which seems to worsen every time he draws a breath.

He had dreaded going to his first class this morning. Not because he dislikes math, but because his two attackers from the previous night would be sitting behind him. But so far the morning had been uneventful, although it's early days. Kurt and Robbie are surprisingly quiet and so far had ignored him.

"Turn to page 28 and 29 of your trigonometry book please. While you're reading over the exercises on those two pages, please have your homework ready for collection. You'll get the homework back on Friday," Mr. Arthur, the math teacher,

shouts to be heard over the noisy students. Moans continue to be heard throughout the class of twenty-eight students. "Stop talking and get reading. Have your homework ready." The teacher is rapidly losing his patience. Underlying mumbles can still be heard, along with the sound of papers being shuffled and book pages being turned. But there is now general order in the classroom.

Paul opens up his trigonometry book and finds the pages concerned. He reaches below his desk and takes a folder out of his carryall. Opening the folder up, he starts to thumb through its contents until he locates his homework. As he's about to remove two sheets of letter paper from their plastic wallet, he suddenly feels something sharp dig into his back. He jumps; the pain from his injured ribs racks his body.

He turns around and looks at his taunter, Kurt. Paul sees that the offending weapon that has been stabbed into his back is a protractor.

"We have some unfinished business my friend." Kurt holds the metal instrument in a threatening manner towards his victim. Paul doesn't respond to the bully's terrorizing words; he turns back to his desk and he flinches as he feels the protractor stab into his back once again. This time however, he's sure it has drawn blood.

"Don't think that by ignoring me I'm going to go away nerd. We can continue our conversation later," whispers Kurt aggressively into Paul's ear.

Paul can feel tears well up in his eyes. He doesn't know how much longer he can cope with this constant intimidation. Absorbed in his own troubles, Paul doesn't notice that there now seems to be an air of excitement amongst his fellow female students.

"Class, I'd like to introduce you to a new student who has joined our school today." Mr. Arthur's words cause the class to fall into silence.

Paul looks up and sees a young man standing beside the

teacher. It's strange but he's sure the new student is surrounded by a faint glow. He blinks and the glow disappears, it must be an illusion caused by the bright sunlight that's streaming through the window.

"Class, meet Daniel Pierce." The math teacher's manner is warm and welcoming.

Paul thinks that the new kid looks friendly enough; he doesn't look mean, but then again appearances can be deceptive. This guy Daniel seems pretty self-assured. Oh God, Paul hopes that he isn't like Kurt.

Chapter Six

Whoever loves discipline loves knowledge, but he who hates correction is stupid.

Proverbs 12:1

Kurt's Story

Kurt notices Jenny's interest in the new boy. After her reluctance to meet up last night, he wonders if she is growing a little tired of him. Not that it will make any difference one way or the other to him. After all, there are plenty more fish in the sea.

He decides it's time for Jenny to prove her love for him. How; he isn't sure. In fact, he has made a few other decisions. For one, it's time that Robbie is rewarded for his loyalty. But most importantly, it's time to sort out that nerd Paul once and for all.

§ § §

That was a *looong* morning, sorry for the yawn. I'm now ravenous. My stomach's making all kinds of echoing sounds. The scrambled eggs and pancakes with maple syrup that Aunt Sylvia made for me this morning have now been fully digested and it's time to top up.

So here I am in line, waiting to be served in the cafeteria. I got a bit lost trying to find my way here, as it's on the other side of school. But eventually I just followed the crowd and I got here. The place is buzzing with kids, just like me, well not exactly like me because it's very unlikely that any others are angelets. But you never know. What I really mean is, they're all extremely hungry.

While I wait, I'm looking around the sea of faces that

fill the room. I'm hoping to pick out a friendly face from class, who hopefully I can sit down beside and eat lunch with.

I'm sliding my lunch tray along the stainless steel runners that are adjacent to the counter, the tray belonging to the guy behind me keeps sliding into mine, and it's now becoming a bit irksome. I don't know if he's trying to provoke me into saying something to him or what, but I'm keeping my mouth tightly closed. I don't want any trouble on my first day.

I look into the first glass display unit; it's crammed with an array of fresh green salads and an assortment of filled baguettes. Mmm, choices, choices. What would you choose?

I can see that there are hot meals being served further up the line by a large, jovial black woman. But I'll stick to the cold stuff; I've decided to opt for a tuna salad. The next unit contains various desserts. I choose a slice of banana cream pie with a dollop of whipped cream on the side; my tray's filling up. Yuck, the cream looks rather unappetizing on this dessert, not sure I should have picked it. I've eaten an awful lot of cream on the side since I've arrived in Wingate. Never mind, I've reached the hot food counter.

"Hi, are you a new kid?" The woman I mentioned before, who's serving, is a real happy sort. You know the type, she laughs and everyone laughs with her.

"Yes I am, for my sins." Why did I say that?

"What's your name?" She chortles.

"Dan." I must say I'm getting used to my name now.

"Dan, hurry up. Dan, new boy, we want to eat too." Some kid behind me in line is getting rather impatient; he's decided to be spokesman for the rest of the kids.

"Don't you worry none about being the new boy, Dan. A good looking boy like you is going to fit right in, here in Wingate," the lunch lady says encouragingly. "And if anyone gives you trouble Dan, come and see your Aunt JoJo. I look after all the new kids." She looks disapprovingly up the line at the grumbling student. Then smiling at me she says, "Now what can I get you?"

"Some French fries please."

"Uh huh, and you've got manners as well boy, you'll fit right in. French fries coming right up." JoJo heaps the fries into a soup bowl, leans over the counter, and puts them on my tray. "Now I've put extra in there for you, young Dan. So don't be wasting them. Eat them and you too can have a figure like me." She laughs loudly. The noise she makes sounds as though it could belong in the hyena enclosure at the zoo. Her large breasts heave and jiggle about as she exhales her laughter.

"Thanks, JoJo." I can feel my face slightly redden with embarrassment on realization that some of the other kids are paying more attention to me than I would like. Of course the fact that I've told you about JoJo's breasts should be the main reason for making me blush. Eek. I quickly move on, grab a medium size cup of cola, and pay for my lunch at the till.

At the first set of tables I reach, the seats are all taken. As I scan my eyes around this vast room, the noise of chatter and the clatter of plates make it hard to take everything in. Great, I can see Paul; I identified him in class. The good news, for me anyway, is that he's sitting all alone.

He's a studious type of dude. I'll ask him if I can join him and take it from there.

I'm making my way through the tables. *Buzzzzz, buzzzzz,* my blasted earring is vibrating in my lobe.

"Hey new boy, Dan, or whatever your name is. Come join us," shouts a male voice. I look to the table on my left, then on my right; no one sitting at either of these tables even acknowledges I'm here. *Buzzzzz, buzzzzz.* Ouch! The stud in my ear has just emitted a small electric shock through my body. A hand grips my elbow from behind. I turn around, wow, what the…?

I've spilled some of my cola onto my tray, not because of the electric charge, but because of what I thought I saw when I first turned around. I was sure the kid I'm facing had a large purple head and horns. Maybe the excitement of the day is causing me to hallucinate. Now that the horns and the strange hue have disappeared, I'm facing quite a handsome looking guy. He's bigger than me, in build and in height. But ladies he is no match to me in the handsome stakes. I jest, he's what you would call tall, dark, and handsome, I suppose.

"Hi, I'm Robbie Dillon. Come join us," he says in a husky voice. He doesn't give me any time to respond, he's expecting me to follow. He moves away from me and squeezes behind the occupants of the table on my left. Out of curiosity I'm following him.

The table he stops at is beside the large glass windows that complete one wall of the room. It has two occupants, one male, the other female. I recognize them as being fellow students in my class. Robbie sits down beside the guy who's already there.

"Sit down, Dan. I'm Kurt Hills and this gorgeous creature is Jenny Green." Kurt Hills points to the empty chair opposite him. Wo…w, there's that hallucination again, now it's both guys. Deep breath, deep breath. Don't panic. Okay, things are back to normal. So this is Jenny. She forces a slight smile, or is it a grimace? I'm not sure what. But at least she's not purple. He's right when he says she's gorgeous. Wah-wee.

"Hi. I see I don't need to introduce myself. I must have made such a good impression when I joined class," I jokingly say. Not one of the threesome even cracks a smile. They don't seem to notice my little joke, then again maybe it was a bit corny.

"Thanks for asking me to join you." Do I sound sincere? Thought not.

"Welcome to Wingate," Robbie says rather unconvincingly. Kurt is now looking at Jenny intently. Her gaze moves nervously from him, to me, then to Robbie.

"Say hello to Dan, Jenny," Kurt demands.

"Hi, Dan," she mumbles. Her eyes drop self-consciously towards the table top.

"Say it as though you mean it." Kurt takes hold of Jenny's hand. His grip is so tight, I can see the color is draining from his knuckles, and the tips of her fingers.

"Hi Dan, nice to meet you." This time Jenny grins and speaks clearly. I want to tell this guy, Kurt, that you don't treat ladies this way. But my instinct tells me that anything I say will be falling on deaf ears. So for now, I'll just go with the flow.

Obviously there's something amiss in this group. Whether it's the whole group, you and I will just need to wait and see. At the risk of repeating myself, I'm famished.

Thank you Lord for this food, for which I am truly thankful. Amen. Let lunch commence.

Chapter Seven

Flee from sexual immorality. All other sins a man commits are outside his body, but he who sins sexually sins against his own body.

1 Corinthians 6:18

Paul's Story

Paul Mitchum is at home in the kitchen, he's pouring a can of soup into a pan when he hears the front door opening. He had arrived home later than usual from school, after having decided to stay on and do some research in the library for his biology project. He excels in sciences and he had hoped that one day he would become a doctor.

But recently he's found it difficult to think about the future in a positive way. He is constantly in fear of his life. If it isn't Kurt and Robbie haranguing him relentlessly, it's his father's violent outbursts towards him.

At that, the kitchen door bursts open and in flounces George Mitchum. Paul takes a deep breath and he says,

"Hi Pop. Do you want me to make you something to eat?"

"No, I don't want anything to eat. I just want a drink." George staggers towards his son.

"Pop, don't you think you've had enough?" Paul looks at his father timidly.

"You need to remember who the parent is around here. If I want a drink, I'll have a drink." George grabs hold of Paul's face, causing Paul to flinch. "Have you been fighting again?"

"No I haven't. I fell." Paul avoids making eye contact with his father; he hates having to lie.

"You fell. Don't make me laugh. Don't lie to me; you fell

into someone's fist. I've told you before; you need to start acting like a man. You should make sure your opponent is the only one that looks as though he's been in a fight. Ha." George slurs some of his words.

"What does acting like a man mean, Pop? Does it mean I should go around beating people up? Or, maybe I should go out and get bombed every night."

Paul feels the full force of his father's fist as George lands a punch on his already injured cheek. The pain surges through Paul's head. He drops to his knees and he begins to cry.

"Cry baby, cry baby," shouts George mockingly. He staggers across the room and he says, "I'm having a beer." He fumbles with the refrigerator door in his desperation to get a drink. Finally, he opens it; the door swings wide, causing the whole fridge to rattle. He takes out a beer and pulls the tab back. In one swift movement, he empties all of the liquid contents into his mouth.

Crushing the spent can in the palm of his hand, he drops it into the soup Paul was preparing. George belches loudly, then takes out another beer and leaves the room, leaving his son lying on the kitchen floor sobbing.

§ § §

Well, that's my first day at Wingate High over. At least I've now put faces to a couple of the people that you and I have been reading about. I can tell you Kurt and Robbie were a real revelation. They're definitely demonlets, no doubt about that. No need to Goddle them. I should explain. Goddle is a heavenly search engine.

Ding, dong. Ding, dong. Hey, that's the doorbell. I'll need to see who's at the door. Aunt Sylvia's out hospital visiting; which she does on a regular basis, for obvious reasons.

"You ready boy?" Isais grins at me as I open the door to him.

"Ready for what?" I have no idea what he's talking about.

"Soccer practice. You're going with me. I coach the local team and I promised Sylvie I'd keep an eye on you."

"Oh Isais, I love soccer but I'm not sure I'd be any good at it."

"Come on boy. This isn't up for discussion. Hell, it doesn't matter if you're good at it. It's about meeting other kids, exercise, and just having fun. It's really catching on and the Olympic Development Program even has scouts visiting soccer clubs and schools throughout Arizona. My boy, Askii, loved it."

"I'll have to look for shorts and athletic shoes, eh, I'm not sure where..." I hope he doesn't look at my feet. I've got athletic shoes on. Whoops.

"No need, Dan. I've got your kit here; Sylvie fixed it out earlier today." My excuse isn't washing with Isais. He taps the large bulging carryall he's holding. He's not going to allow me to become a couch potato for sure. If Aunt Sylvia's arranged this, I'm positive there's a purpose for me going along. Then again she maybe just doesn't want me to get fat with all her pies. Do angelets get fat? Answers by email please.

"Then let's go score some goals." I'm trying to sound enthusiastic.

§ § §

Jenny's Story

Jenny is sitting at her bedroom window, looking out at nothing in particular. She can hear her mother, Gabriella, in the shower. She must be going out again with Andy. She hopes she's taking Kushi with her.

Jenny's mind had been in turmoil since setting eyes on the new guy, Dan Pierce. She had wanted to be friendly to him, but she didn't know how Kurt would react. She had been somewhat bewildered by Kurt's amicable demeanor at lunchtime. He didn't normally welcome guys into his fold so readily, especially good looking ones, and Dan Pierce was precisely that.

The minute he walked into class, Jenny's stomach had started to somersault. Then there was the tingling that stirred deep down inside her. She used to get that same feeling when Kurt kissed her, but she didn't feel it anymore.

Jenny knew by her fellow female student's reactions that Dan had the same effect on them. There was something special about him. Although she couldn't quite say what.

It was strange, but she was convinced for a moment that Dan had been surrounded by a bright light when she had first seen him. But when she blinked the light had vanished. It was like a dream sequence in a movie.

It wasn't only his looks she found attractive. His voice seemed to have this kind of hypnotic quality. The saying 'voice of an angel' came to mind, but she was sure that was a reference to someone's singing voice.

Jenny jumps nearly out of her skin at the sound of music she hears coming from her cell. She has an incoming text. She looks at the screen and opens the message. It reads, I have a surprise for you. My house tonight 7:30 and make sure you wear those undies I like. What kind of surprise could Kurt have for her? It was no surprise to her that he wanted to make out, that's why he would refer to her undies. But what?

"Please don't let him have the keys to his Dad's car again. Not after that last time." She speaks aloud in her anguish.

§ § §

Demonlets at Work

"Oh Satan, we applaud thee. We are ready to carry out your work. Give us the power to torment the righteous, we beseech thee. We are your servants on this earth. We will destroy, in your name Satan, all that is good. Send us the lambs to

slaughter." The two young men stand in front of the mirror, awaiting their transformation.

The room fills with a red glow, they look at their reflections, but they are unrecognizable. Their purple faces are distorted. The saliva drips from their lion-like fangs. Their forward arcing tails are completed by a venomous telson.

"Satan, Satan, Satan," they chant loudly.

Smoke fills the room. The air becomes heavy with a musky aroma. Their images are no longer reflected in the mirror. The frame comes to life and now they can see their idol. The red dragon's seven heads, with their ten pointed horns, move erratically.

"You have called and I grant you the power to torment. Rid me of the righteous and moral. Be my faithful servants. For I welcome you into my world." Each mouth moves in synchronization.

"Kurt, your dad and I are going out now and for God's sake, turn that music down," calls out Mrs. Hills from elsewhere in the house.

Chapter Eight

Be still before the LORD and wait patiently for him; do not fret when men succeed in their ways, when they carry out their wicked ways, when they carry out their wicked schemes.

Psalm 37:7

Last night was an eye opener, to say the least. I don't know why I'm surprised. Sorry, you don't have a clue what I'm talking about; soccer. Yeah, yeah, yeah. I'm still going on about soccer.

Well, what I do need to tell you is I'm absolutely ace at footie, as the British would call it. You're wondering how I know they call it footie. Well I don't know. Eh, maybe I drifted across the Atlantic on a sail boat, on the crest of a wave, so to speak.

Okay, okay, I'm just fooling. I don't know. I'm just using a bit of poetic license. Anyway, forget all the junk I've just spouted. Hey, the piece about me being ace isn't junk. That's the truth, so help me God.

§ § §

Jenny's Story

Jenny's mind is in a whirl. She doesn't have any idea what went on when she went over to Kurt's last night. She's not even sure if she went. But if she hadn't he would have sent her a nasty text, and he hadn't. What she does know is that she had a terrible nightmare. She's never been so frightened in her life.

Both Kurt and Robbie were in her dream. She was sure it was them anyway. They were unrecognizable. It was their voices that she had recognized. They were both some kind of purple monsters, spitting fire. She had been forced to make out with both of them.

Ugh, she just wanted to blot it out of her mind. But the vision just wouldn't go away, it was so vivid. It was as though her dream had been reality.

§ § §

Paul's Story

Paul had been avoiding his Gran the last few days. He knew she would be terribly upset if she saw the state he was in. He couldn't continue telling her and his teachers that he kept walking into doors, or tripping up. No one was that clumsy.

So last night in bed after the terrible nightmare he had about Kurt and Robbie, he had made a decision. The decision was life changing. He knew the outcome would upset his gran, but he didn't think it would make any difference to his dad. He thought it would be better for everyone all round.

Because of his injuries he was exempt from taking part in the PE class today. The teacher said he could do some research on Native North American sports instead and report back with his findings. He thought he'd write about Lacrosse. Heck, what does it matter what he writes about.

Paul pulls out some books from his school locker, closes the door, and locks it. He reads the words on the door that are written in black felt tip pen, NERD YOUR TIME HAS COME. No prizes as to guessing whose handy work it is. The teenager sighs, but the words don't really disturb him too much this morning. The reason being, he is going to his favorite place in the entire school, the library. It's his place of refuge, his shelter from harm's way, his place of solitude, and the only spot in the whole wide world he feels safe. He has a lot to think through. He looks at his watch, he better get a move on, or he'll be late.

Paul walks across the large grassy area to the front of the main building, his books are neatly tucked underneath his arm. The strong sun beats down onto his bare arms; he looks up towards the sky, there's not a cloud to be seen. Hopefully this means there would be no thunderstorms today, as is prevalent to Scottsdale in July.

§ § §

Fun, fun, fun, that's what I'm about to have. I've escaped the crowded hallways inside school and I'm outside in the central courtyard. I need to make my way to the playing fields for PE class and this is a shortcut. Hey, take a guess what we're doing today. You got it in one: soccer. I've heard that I'll have a bit of stiff competition, because it seems that demonlet, Kurt Hills, is the school's most promising all round athlete and is a star at soccer.

Hey, it's only a game. If he's better than me I won't get bent out of shape about it, that's for sure. *Buzzzzz, buzzzz.*

"Dan, wait for us," shouts someone. I turn around, what the...? Talking of bent out of shape, I'm getting those weird images again as well as being zapped by a gold stud. All I can see is fangs and big tails and I mean biiig tails. Deep breath, deep breath.

"Hi Kurt, hi Robbie. Didn't hear you sneaking up behind me." I'm trying to act cool. Blink, blink, and blink. They're still looking real weird. I hope Aunt Sylvia hasn't put some strange hallucinogenic plant in her pies by mistake. Okay, normal vision resumes.

"Are you going to soccer too?" asks Kurt.

"Yes, I most definitely am."

"Have you played much?" He's acting real amicably.

"Eh, well I played last night. A friend of my aunt coaches a small team, Wingate Rams. You may know him, if you're into soccer, his name's Isais. He had a kid our age that died in an automobile accident some months ago."

"No, we don't know him. There's a few small soccer teams around. But the players aren't up to much. They're just not up to our standard." Kurt shakes his head, Robbie stays silent. Kurt seems to be answering on behalf of both of them. I can't have that; I'm going to challenge this dude's silence.

"What about you, Robbie? Did you know the kid, or do you know his dad?" I look Robbie straight in the eye. He looks at Kurt for some kind of support.

"I told you Dan, we don't know either of them." Kurt quickly comes to his aid.

"Cat got your tongue, Robbie?" I keep looking at Robbie, ignoring Kurt's comments.

"As Kurt said, we don't know them. Don't socialize with injuns." Robbie finally finds his tongue and he smiles wryly. Kurt casts an uneasy glance at Robbie.

"If you don't know anything about Isais, what's with the bigoted remark?" Of course I now know that Robbie should be called Pinocchio, because of that big fat lie he just told. Kurt looks angry, his cheeks have a kind of pink tinge to them. Let's hope that he and Robbie aren't about to turn purple again.

"What's with all the questions, Dan? We told you, we don't know them. Come on, Dan; let's see if you're as good at soccer as you are at being nosey." Kurt's becoming very defensive, it's time to change tactics.

"I'm better." I laugh. The two guys look at each other and start to laugh. Now all three of us are laughing. But I've hit on something that these two don't want to share and I don't think it's a laughing matter.

I hear footsteps coming up from behind. Turning around I see that it's Paul.

"Hi Paul, you want to walk with us?" My offer, I can see, isn't appreciated by Paul, the color has just drained from his face. In the blink of an eye, Robbie pivots around. Oh, once more Kurt and Robbie are looking very strange.

"Where you going nerd?" Robbie's the first to speak. Paul doesn't answer, he keeps on walking. The kid looks awful, but not half as awful as these two creatures that have replaced Kurt and Robbie. The good thing is Paul doesn't see them as I do, nevertheless Paul is terrified. I need to do something or at least say something.

"Catch up with you another time Paul." I'm trying to pretend they look normal to me, I don't want to blow my cover. Paul gives me a nervous kind of smile. He's passing us; anything could happen now. Yep, the anything is happening. That big scorpion tail belonging to Robbie is curving right over his head and aiming straight for Paul. A picture flashes into my head of Paul lying slumped on the grass with blood pouring from his head.

Focus, focus, focus and I pray inwardly. I can feel a strange sensation push through my body. Robbie plans to trip Paul up, without a doubt his intention is to hurt him. If Paul falls onto the stone edging that borders the flower beds, it could result in some really serious damage.

I'm concentrating real hard; I'm having some type of out of body experience. I'm still standing here, but a bright silhouette has surged out of my body and grasped the threatening telson belonging to Robbie. I'm pulling it back, back, and back. I can feel the power I'm exerting drain my body. The stinger can no longer reach Paul. Paul hurries on, he's out of danger.

Thump, Robbie falls to the ground. I'm me again, but I feel jaded. I look at Kurt and Robbie, they're returning to their human forms.

"Get up Robbie and leave it for now," Kurt says angrily.

"Must've lost my footing." Robbie looks kind of bewildered.

"You okay Robbie?" I ask innocently. "You need to

watch what you're doing dude."

Kurt and Robbie look at each other in puzzlement.

"Yes he does need to watch what he's doing. He needs to keep himself in one piece if he's going to play well at soccer," says Kurt calmly.

Oh, oh. No monsters this time, but up ahead I see the PE teacher whose silhouette somewhat resembles that of a grizzly bear. He's waving his huuuge arms and pointing to his watch. I think maybe we're late for soccer. God give me some strength, because I'm done in after my little adventure. Wait until I tell Aunt Sylvia.

Chapter Nine

Have no fear of sudden disaster or of the ruin that overtakes the wicked, for the LORD will be your confidence and will keep your foot from being snared.

Proverbs 3:25, 26

What's my other favorite pastime? Food. It's that time again, lunch awaits. Jekyll and Hyde, the gruesome twosome, say they're going to Kurt's for lunch today. They asked me to go with them, but to be pretty honest I don't really think they're the kind of company your mom, or my Aunt Sylvia, would want us to be associating with. So I politely declined the invitation.

As you know I'm new at this game of being an angelet, and God, whatever version you believe in, likes to find redeeming qualities in each and every one of us, but so far I haven't spotted theirs. Have you?

Sooo, I need to seek out some new friends and where better to do that than in the cafeteria. It's the same old story in any high school restaurant in the western world: wait in line, grab a tray, look into the glass cabinets to see if anything takes your fancy, pop the plate on your tray, pay for it, hope you're really going to enjoy it, munch through it, and then biiig decision time. Did you actually enjoy it? Decisions, decisions.

In the chilled cabinets, I can't see anything that will appease my hunger today. I think I'll need to opt for one of the culinary delights from the hot food counter. It's that nice lady JoJo who's serving.

"Hi JoJo, what do you recommend for a hungry soul today?" There I go again with all those religious words.

"Dan, nice to see you again. Are you enjoying yourself?" She's so warm and friendly.

"Yes I am, very much so, JoJo. Everybody is so friendly here." Okay, I lied a teeny bit.

"I saw you've been hanging out with Kurt and Robbie, they are two good boys. You're lucky to have them as your friends." She sounds so sincere. It's a surprise to me that anyone would recommend them as friends.

"Well we're not bosom pals as yet. Early days." And they're never likely to be. Alarm bells are ringing in my head; but no earring buzzing. She's now looking pretty serious.

"They could be your best friends if you let them young Dan. Pretty boys should all hang out together," she says unsmiling.

"I like them JoJo and as I said, early days. They might not want me as a friend, they're quite inseparable." I'm thinking this conversation is a bit heavy to be having over hot food trays. I can hear mumbling behind me from the others waiting in line and so can JoJo.

"Well young Dan, how about some lasagna?" She's lightened up.

"Yes, thanks JoJo, it looks real appetizing." Sorry God, I just fibbed. I don't feel so hungry now after my little talk.

I actually feel as though there's some kind of disturbing warning hidden in JoJo's words. Pretty boy indeed. I need to Goddle search her later. Last time I tried, I thought my tablet was going to explode.

§ § §

Jenny's Story

"Hey Jen, where's lover boy today?" Suzie Kowalski and several other of Jenny's girlfriends are huddled round one of the larger tables in the school cafeteria. The girls spend their lunch breaks looking around at the male population of the school and gossiping about fellow senior's love lives.

Jenny hadn't noticed her friends and her face lights up with a welcoming smile when she hears the friendly voice. She pulls up a chair and squeezes her tray onto the already crammed table top. The other occupants at the table shuffle around to give her a bit more room, they all smile, and await her answer.

"Oh Kurt, Robbie, and some of the other guys have gone to Kurt's for lunch."

"Must be a male bonding thing then," says Suzie. The other girls giggle and make noises of agreement. But Jenny doesn't see the funny side of Suzie's comment, because she was sure there was a hint of cattiness in her friend's remark.

"Don't know what it is, but I'm glad to get a bit of breathing space," says Jenny. Her friends look from one to another, they can't believe their ears.

"Are things cooling between you and him then?" asks Suzie boldly. Jenny doesn't respond; she stares into her cup of cola. "Jenny, has something gone wrong between you and Kurt?" Suzie glances quickly around the table at the other four girls and she raises her eyebrows. She uses the visual expression as though it were to communicate some secret code between the girls.

"No I just had a bad night. Strange nightmares. In fact I'm pretty shook up." Jenny looks up from her drink and she swallows hard. A sigh of relief can be heard from each of her girlfriends.

"Thank God for that. We thought you and Kurt were on the verge of breaking up or something. Didn't we girls?" Suzie carries on as the main spokesperson for the group.

"Yes, we did," all the girls speak together and nod.

"For goodness sakes, Jenny, act your age. Imagine allowing bad dreams to upset your whole day," says Suzie dismissively.

"I know, but I'm not sure if it was a dream, that's the problem." Jenny looks back at her cup. Suzie starts to laugh, so do the others at the table. Just as she is about to say something else about Jenny's dream, Suzie notices Dan as he goes by.

More nudges and facial expressions pass among the females at the table.

"I don't know about dreams, but there is one dream that's just walked by. He's gorgeous. Mmm, mmm." Suzie's gaze follows Dan.

"Oh, that's Dan, isn't he an absolute angel?" Jenny looks up and smiles cutely.

"You better not let Kurt hear you say that," giggles Suzie.

"What did I say?" Jenny looks surprised. She takes a fleeting look at her friend's faces and fits of giggles erupt in the group.

"Have you spoken to him Jenny?" Suzie wants to hear more.

"Yes, Kurt called him over yesterday. He sat with us at lunch."

"Well Jenny, do your duty, go get him over here girl, and introduce us to him."

The noise of excitement that's being vocalized amongst the girlfriends sounds like a gaggle of geese.

"Oh, I don't know about that. I didn't speak much to him at all and I don't know what Kurt would say," says Jenny hesitantly.

"What Kurt doesn't know won't harm him. Anyway, it's not you that wants to sit with him, it's the rest of us. We'll take the blame. Go on," says Suzie coaxingly, and she pushes Jenny slightly on the back.

"Go on," plead the rest of the girls.

Jenny stands up and starts walking slowly up the aisle between the banks of tables. She stops, turns around, and looks back at her girlfriends. They all start waving their arms, urging her on. She pulls herself up to her full height, she runs her tongue over her lips, her hands smooth over her long blonde hair, and this time she needs no coaxing.

§ § §

I've just passed the giggling girls. It seems I'm rather popular with the senior girls, but as you know they're totally barking up the wrong tree. It's a pity because some of them are pretty hot and that includes Jenny. Sorry God. I'll try and keep my mind on the matters at hand.

"Hi Paul, can I sit here?" I've found the table I was looking for. Paul Mitchum looks up from the book he's reading.

"You can if you want, I'll finish and let you have the table." He looks rather ashen faced. Ghost like. No, not like me, I'm not a ghost. I need to put this kid at ease, let him know I'm not his enemy.

"Paul, I don't want you to leave. I want to get to know you."

"Is this some kind of wind up? Did Kurt send you?" Paul stands up and starts to gather up his belongings, dropping books and papers onto the floor in his rush. I put my tray down onto the table, I get down onto my knees, and I start picking his books up. He tries to pull the books out of my hands. I try and grip onto them real tight, but it's difficult because he's a big kid.

"Paul, I want to be your friend."

"Why?" He sounds upset.

"Because I think you need one."

Paul lets go of his grip on his books, thuds down into his chair, and I put his things onto the table.

"Shake on being friends Paul." I stretch out my hand to him. I can see he's not too sure what to do. However he's giving me a smile of sorts and he shakes my hand. I feel a strange sensation in my arm, in fact through my body. It's as though power is leaving my body and traveling down my arm into Paul. He's oblivious to it that's for sure. I have no idea what's happening, do you? Answers by email.

"Friends," says Paul and he relaxes. I can safely sit down opposite him now he's going nowhere. Anyway I'm starrrving. I look at the lasagna that's lying in a blob on the plate. It looks stodgy, I know it will be tasteless. Does moving it about the plate with my fork make it taste any better, do you think?

"So Paul what..." Before I can finish my sentence, I feel a hand on my shoulder. The soft touch sends a tingle through my body. I turn to see Jenny standing beside me.

"Dan, do you want to come and sit with us?" She isn't forcing a smile today. She has a lovely smile. I think my mind's slipping into dangerous territory, for an angelet anyway.

"Yes, that would be great. We'll be over in a moment." I'm grinning like a right twerp. I don't think she was expecting me to say that. Don't ask me what I thought she was expecting to say, because I don't know. But I just have a gut feeling.

"Okay in a moment," says Jenny. She wavers for a second, then she looks from me to Paul and she smiles. Wow, what a smile. She walks away, I put my cutlery and plate of stodgy lasagna back onto my tray, and I stand up to follow.

"Well Dan, I'll see you around," says Paul sadly.

"What do you mean you'll see me around? You don't think I can handle all those chicks on my own. You're coming with me."

"Oh Dan, why would you want me there? I'll cramp your style."

"Paul, you won't cramp my style; you're my friend." Little does he know my style's already more than a little cramped.

Chapter Ten

Are not all angels ministering spirits sent to serve those who will inherit salvation?

Hebrews 1:14

Demonlet Story

"Satan, Satan, we applaud thee."

Kurt, Robbie, and two other new recruits from the school soccer team, Steven and Barry, chant to their satanic idol. Kurt's bedroom is filled with a blaze of red light and the atmosphere hangs heavy with the aroma of sulfur.

All four of the young men transmute into purple monsters. Their scorpion like tails bend over their heads and sway. The pincers that have replaced their arms pinch the air and the sacrificial lamb's blood glistens as it drips from their front teeth.

"We serve thee, we serve thee. Empower us, empower us," they repeat in a monotone drone. The room plunges into darkness and flashes of crimson light echoes around the room. The foursome continue to recite their words of reverence, "Oh tormentor we worship you. Oh tormentor we worship you." The revelers fall to their knees as the red dragon reveals himself through a white cloud of smoke.

"You applaud me. You worship me. But you do not serve me. You have welcomed a servant of the lamb of God into your lives. He's being allowed to go about his business of righteousness and you make no attempt to stop him. I cannot welcome you to sit by me when you have fallen at the first hurdle," he ridicules. The heat in the room is intense from the fire that's spurting from the mouths of the spirit of evil. The devil worshippers gasp at his spoken words and are surprised

as well as disappointed when he vanishes.

But the boys are unaware of the presence of another human in the house and they don't hear the noise of footsteps coming up the stairs. Tap, tap, tap, tap, the bedroom door is being knocked.

"Kurt, did you and your friends eat those lamb chops I left out for tea? Or was it the dog, because I notice there's no dirty pan? Kurt, do you hear me?" Kurt's mom sounds puzzled. "Kurt, unlock this door. I won't have you and your friends smoking dope in this house. My God what a smell. Kurt, Kurt open up," shouts Mrs. Hills and she begins to rattle the door handle violently.

§ § §

That's my school day over, time to head home and have some foood. I arranged to meet up with Paul at the main door. The two of us can walk home together. He's a real nice guy and once he got over his initial shyness with the girls earlier at lunch time, he had them eating out of his hand, so to speak. In fact, he has quite a way with the ladies.

He's waiting for me right now, and he's chatting with Suzie and Jenny. How do I know this? Well it's not some magical angelic power I possess. I can see them up ahead. Ha, ha, caught you. They look like they're having fun. Probably a lot of flirting going on.

They've spotted me and the girls are grinning from ear to ear. Did I tell you before my hairstyle is a hit with the ladies? You should get one; that's if you're a dude. It's not a style I would recommend for girls. Though each to their own.

Sorry, I digress. Hey, Paul's smiling too and that's good, because he doesn't seem to do that very often. How do I know that? Well, I read the same stuff as you.

"Hi, thanks for waiting Paul. Nice to see you girls again." The girl's are real cute.

"No problem Dan. Suzie's going to walk home with us," says Paul.

"Great, what about you Jenny? You live nearby to me, don't you?" My attention on Jenny seems to be making her blush. Heck is she blushing. Wow. She looks like one of those sun blushed tomatoes.

"I'd like to Dan, but Kurt wouldn't like me to. So I'd better not," she stammers slightly.

"So he's one of those jealous types, is he?" I know the answer, but I'm trying to make conversation here, so forgive me.

"Yes he is a bit." She's still stammering and her face is now like Rudolf's nose. Bright red. "A bit. He'd go mad; in fact he is mad, but that's another story." The hesitation has now gone from Jenny's voice.

"Never mind her Dan; you've got me to walk home with," interrupts Suzie, laughing forcefully. Paul coughs. "And Paul of course." Remembers Suzie. She's a real good-looking girl, is Suzie. She's what you would describe as kind of sassy. Her shoulder length brown hair, dark brown eyes, and… oh, oh, need to get my mind back on track. She is sassy though. Sorry God, for that wayward slip.

"Well another time perhaps Jenny." I try to sound let down by her decision. I touch her arm gently; I'm practicing that touch of an angel thing again.

"Yes, I will walk with you. Kurt needs to grow up." Jenny now appears relaxed. Suzie is trying to look pleased that Jenny is coming with us. But I can see a green eyed monster at work. I said green, not purple, so don't worry. Not yet anyway.

§ § §

Something really strange happened on the way home, I forgot about my stomach being empty. I think it was because I was enjoying the company of my newfound friends. Suzie kept everyone amused with her tittle-tattle. Of which I didn't take any part in. Eh, what I'm trying to explain is that I was amused, but angelets don't do gossip. Okay glad I cleared that up; I'll continue.

She was also trying very hard to become my sweetheart. I think maybe that terminology is passé, but hey, I'm passé, I'm dead. So forgive me if I don't always use fashionable figures of speech. Putting it plain and simply; she just fell short of asking me for a date.

She's not the shy and retiring type by any manner of means. So once she gets to know me better, she probably will. Therefore tomorrow I can expect her to ask me out. Ha, ha. It's not that I don't find her attractive, but…

I think Jenny is my type, that's if I wasn't an angelet. Oh, oh, it's dangerous territory time again. It's her pale blue eyes and her sun-kiss… Enough said, fill in the blanks yourself.

I'm home and I can smell something real good. I'm meeting up with Paul later and I'll catch up with you then because it's foood, foood.

Chapter Eleven

The eyes of the LORD are on the righteous and his ears are attentive to their prayer, but the face of the LORD is against those who do evil.

Psalm 34:15,16

Jenny's Story

Jenny's unbuttoning her blouse; she's changing out of her school clothes. She's going to have a shower then change into something more comfortable. Hearing her cell phone ring, she goes over to the dresser where it's lying on top. Looking at the display, she's surprised to see that it's Suzie calling. She sits down on the edge of her bed and she pushes the call answer key.

"Hi Suzie, what's up?"

"What do you think my chances are of Dan asking me out on a date, Jen?" asks Suzie in an excited tone.

"You're keen. You've really got the hots for him, haven't you?" Jenny is taken aback by her friend's revelation.

"He's one of the cutest guys I've seen in a long time and I want him to be mine," says Suzie willfully.

"Well Suzie, he seems to like you," says Jenny encouragingly.

"I don't just want him to like me. I want him to have the hots for me, the same way I have for him."

"Suzie, he's just met you. You know what some guys are like, they're a bit on the slow side when it comes to asking girls out. Once he knows you better he'll realize how you feel and there will be no stopping him." Jenny continues with her words of encouragement.

"Jen, if he says anything to you about me, drop him a hint that I'd like to go out. Please, please, pretty please," begs Suzie.

"What makes you think that he would discuss anything like that with me?"

"I'm not sure. But I think he's friendlier towards you than he is me. Oh, I don't know; I just want you to help me out here."

"Suzie, maybe he's more relaxed in my company because he doesn't have a crush on me. Perhaps that's because it's you he has a crush on. But, I promise if the opportunity does arise, I will drop him a hint. Although I do think it's unlikely I'll see him alone. You know as well as I do that Kurt won't take too kindly to me being over friendly with him."

"You're such a good friend; I love you," gushes Suzie.

"Listen Suzie I'm going to have to go, Mom's calling me." Jenny makes up an excuse to terminate the call. She's bored with Suzie's childish pining.

"Okay, see you tomorrow and remember, a small hint, or even a large hint at any opportunity. Bye." Suzie makes a last-ditch appeal to her friend.

"Okay, okay. Bye Suzie." Jenny is annoyed at her friend's persistence. But why does she feel jealous of Suzie's attraction to Dan?

§ § §

Isais came in unexpectedly just after I got home from school and is having dinner with us. Aunt Sylvia hasn't said much over dinner; in fact none of us have. I've a feeling she's got something on her mind. I can't ask her what's wrong, or tell her about my day until we're alone. I'm hoping that I haven't done something sinful and I'm about to be red carded.

Sorry about the soccer lingo. In the game, red carded means sent off the playing field. But in angelet terms it means being sent to join the man downstairs, in hell. That's when he's captured and returned home, that is.

"Young Dan how would you like to go to the Rock

'n' Roll Classic Car Show on Saturday afternoon?" The silence is broken by Isais.

"What is it?" I have no idea what he's going on about.

"It's a classic car and motorcycle show held at Scottsdale Pavilions. They showcase several hundred cars, as well as over a hundred or so motorcycles. I know you're into Rock music, but they play some good old fashioned 50's rock 'n' roll music there. Your feet will never stop tapping. I'll teach you what real music is all about," enthuses Isais.

"I'm not sure Isais." I don't want to let him down, but I don't know if it's my kind of thing. Then again, what is my kind of thing? I shouldn't knock it until I've tried it.

"It's a great day out. It doesn't cost anything to go along and we can go pick up some inexpensive food at a diner. There's lots of places that sell filled tacos, flat breads or tortillas, and a great assortment of sides. Is that okay with you Sylvie?" He'd make a great salesman. He could sell ice to the Eskimos.

"Yes you boys go along and have a good time. You should ask your new friend Paul to go along." Aunt Sylvia has just proven that angels don't have secrets, because I haven't even told her about Paul yet.

"Would that be okay Isais, if I ask Paul to come along?"

"Sure, the more the merrier."

"Great. I'll ask him tonight. I'm meeting up with him in an hour at Henry's Pharmacy." I look at my watch, and see that I'm not meeting him in an hour, but in ten minutes. "I didn't realize it was so late. I'll need to shoot, is that cool Aunt Sylvia?" I hate to be rude, but I need to get going.

"Of course it is, you have a good time. We'll catch up later; be careful." There's a note of concern in her voice.

"Go get ready boy I'll give you a ride," says Isais

jovially. He slaps my hand, urging me to hurry up.

"Thanks Isais, I don't want to keep him waiting." I definitely don't. Anything could happen, I can feel it in my bones.

§ § §

Paul's Story

Paul looks at his watch, it's seven o'clock. He shouldn't have bothered hurrying, Dan isn't even here yet. He's glad he had suggested going out for an ice-cream tonight, because it had been extremely hot today. The temperature had probably been around one hundred and five degrees earlier in the day, and it was still very warm. His mouth waters at the thought of the fantastic tutti-frutti nut sundaes the ice-cream parlor does.

He looks down the street, and to his dismay he recognizes the figures walking towards him. He wishes Dan would hurry up. Paul decides to call his new friend on his cell phone, and see if he's nearby; he prays that he is.

No answer, just his voice mail. Desperation is beginning to consume him. The four boys are starting to run towards him; they're coming closer and closer. Paul looks around for somewhere to hide; he supposes he could run into the parlor, but he doesn't want to cause a scene. He has to face up to the situation he now finds himself in; there's nowhere to hide.

Paul tries to move but he's paralyzed, he's firmly stuck to the spot. There's a bright light blinding him; he can't see. What's happening? He feels nauseous, he can hear the sound of blood rushing inside his head. His whole body is numb.

§ § §

Isais and I were on our way to meet Paul when I was first made aware of my big buddy's predicament. But it didn't take me long to release myself into my dust like metaphor, I'm really starting to get the knack of it.

I've arrived at the scene, and there's no time to chat.

Because I'm now made up of moving particles, I'm able to lengthen my reach. So with one celestial beam, I've surrounded the four purple guys with my left arm. I'm pulling the motley bunch together, tight, like a lasso around a steer's neck.

I'm aiming to pluck each demonlet out, one by one, in a hope that I can knock the fight out of them. Divide and conquer is what they call this technique, I believe. Okay, here goes. Numero uno, he's a slippery creature. He's wriggling like bait on a fish hook, but I've managed to restrain him. I throw him hard onto the ground, he won't be bothering me for some time. Numero dos, here goes; that's him down, easy peasy. Numero tres and yes, down he crashes. Numero quatro, I don't think he's sure what's happening. Yes, away we go. All four of them are floored. I punch the air in jubilation, my multi-tasking skills are improving.

Whoa, but these guys don't give up easily. They've all managed to get to their feet and they're rushing towards me. They're trying to grasp me with their pedipalps, but the particles I'm made up of makes it difficult for them to keep track of me, never mind catch me.

The purple creatures are making loud rasping noises. I'll have to use a different tactic if I'm going to win this battle. Here we go again, one of them is fiercely charging towards me. I've caught hold of him. The others have regrouped. They're getting ready for another attack.

I'm encircling them. "Come join your buddy." I'm revolving this little group anti-clockwise, they're still snapping at the air. One of the pincers goes through my arm. But no worries, my particles have readjusted back into place.

Whoooa, the purple dudes are getting dizzy, dizzy, so dizzy. I'm spinning them like tops. Oh, they're crashing into each other and they've collapsed to the ground. High five; reeesult.

The demonlets are moaning and groaning, their strength has totally depleted. *Bang,* they vanish in a puff of smoke. That trick's a new one on me. But I've no time to worry about it, I need to speed up and join my physical being. My body and Isais have just arrived outside the drugstore.

That's me back inside my handsome human form and I jump out of the truck.

"Paul, are you okay dude? Come on big guy." I'm crouching down beside him. Poor kid, he's out cold. He'll be okay, trust me. I'm no doctor, but as you already know I'm an angelet. Isais has joined me, and he's down on his knees on the other side of my buddy. He's moving Paul into the recovery position. I couldn't do that in my Homo sapiens state, because Paul is a big lad, and I'm kind of a weakling. He's now in safe hands, Isais will fix him up.

"Come on, Paul, speak to me boy." Isais is pinching Paul's cheeks gently. Hopefully he'll regain consciousness real soon.

Whilst Isais is in charge of the proceedings, it gives me a chance to catch my breath. This angel lark is quite a tricky business you know. The run in I've just had with the Red Riders entourage was a teeny bit scary.

I wasn't too sure as to what the outcome was going to be. Four against one isn't very good odds, but I'm learning about my non-physical strength all of the time. One minute I was in the truck with Isais, the next I was out strutting my stuff.

"What happened?" Paul's speech is slow but at least he's come round. Things are looking good, he's opened his eyes wide.

"You must have fainted boy. It's pretty warm tonight. Come on, do you think you can get up on your own steam?" Isais offers him his hand.

"Yes." Paul grips onto Isais. I take hold of his free hand, as if to steady him, but I'm hoping my touch will help him.

"Sorry I was late. Let me introduce you to Isais." No time like the present to get the formalities over with. Paul smiles and nods towards Isais in acknowledgment of my introduction.

"Come on, I'm sure Isais will give you a lift home and we can have that ice-cream another time." I don't think Paul is fit to stay out. He's up on his feet, he's none the worse for his ordeal, but he should go home.

"Come on boy, let's get you home to your parents." Isais puts his arm around Paul's torso.

"No I'm not going home. It's just my pop there and he'll be drunk. I'll be okay, if you want to go." Paul shakes his head exaggeratedly. Isais and I are rather taken aback by Paul's outburst.

"Paul, we'll have the ice-cream another night. Come on, surely you'd be better at home?" I need to try to calm the dude down.

"No I'm not going. Just leave me alone," says Paul defiantly; tears are welling up in his eyes.

"Okay boy, you don't need to go home if you don't want to. But how about you and young Dan here come home to my place? I've got some great ice-cream in the freezer. It's the best," says Isais zealously.

"I'd like that, thanks." Paul nods in agreement; thank goodness that's been sorted out. I don't think my metamorphosis could wrestle anymore tonight, I'm worn out.

Chapter Tweleve

"I made a covenant with my eyes not to look lustfully at a girl."

Job 31:1

Wah-wee. Got into some deep conversation with Aunt Sylvia last night about the Red Rider, and his followers. I think she felt I had been holding out on her just a bit. We discussed my latest… I'm not sure what to call it. I think I'll call it my recent dalliance with danger.

But she's feeling a whole lot happier now that she realizes I'm not as green as I'm grass looking. Ooops, I said that incorrectly. I meant to say, not as green as I'm cabbage looking. Now I don't want to hear any more smarty pants remarks from you.

You'll also be glad to hear that Paul is okay after his dalliance with danger last night. Isais took him home after our date with some suuuperb ice-cream. I think he was glad to go, because Isais and I started to talk about the rules of soccer. A discussion that got very animated on occasions. Everything in the end turned out hunky-dory.

Heck, what time is it? I'm laaate for soccer. God, could you beam me into class? I think the fact that I'm running through campus in my human form means that my request has been denied. See you later.

§ § §

Jenny's Story

Jenny pulls her knees up into her chest. She's lying curled up in the fetal position on top of her bed. A light breeze, blowing in through the open bedroom window, billows the voile curtains gently into the room. Her eyes are closed but she isn't asleep. Sleep is the last thing she wants to contemplate after the nightmare she had again last night. Those purple things, ugh.

She isn't going into school today. She told her mom that she had stomach cramps, and Gabriella agreed to call into school for her. Jenny's in the house alone now as her mother has gone to work. But even being alone in daylight hours is beginning to scare her.

Jenny can hear another text coming in on her cell phone, no doubt it will be Kurt. At least he can't call her, because school has strict rules about the use of phones during school hours and texting is easier to conceal.

She starts to think about Dan. Why on earth can't she stop thinking about him? She has never felt this way about any boy, other than Kurt. He's made her realize being with Kurt is a mistake.

Oh, she wishes Dan had never come to the school. Maybe that's why she's having these terrible dreams. That's it; she's just guilty over how she feels about him and it's sending her in a spin. It must be guilt. That's it; guilt.

The bedroom door is slightly ajar; it slams suddenly, and then the door begins to rattle violently. Jenny jumps up and looks around, her eyes open wide with fear. A strong gust of wind comes in through the window causing the curtains to hit repeatedly off the dresser in front of it, and she can hear Kushi yowl downstairs.

"Leave me alone, go away," she shouts, hanging onto her bed as the wind whistles round the room, making her bed shake. The wind dies and Kushi falls silent. Jenny apprehensively looks around the room. Everything is in order; everything is calm, with the exception of Jenny.

§ § §

Wah-hey, I've been picked for the school soccer team. Coach says I have a natural talent. I don't know about that, it's more likely to be a supernatural one. Suzie is sitting with a few girls from class in the cafeteria, they all giggle when they catch sight of me approaching.

"Hey Dan, congratulations," says Suzie sassily. Told you she was sassy.

"Thanks Suzie, I'm really pleased with my news." You know I've just noticed that she's rather well endowed on top. It must be that tight fitting top. Oh, oh dangerous talk. Sorry God.

"Want to come sit with us?"

"Eh, no disrespect, but I want to sit with Paul and talk about boy stuff."

"Like girls?"

"No, actually, soccer."

"Football, or baseball maybe, but soccer?"

"See you later Suzie. I think we meet up in drama class, don't we?"

"Yes we do," she says enthusiastically.

"Well that's a date then Suzie." I can be sassy too, when I want.

"Yes, that's a date Dan." Suzie blushes slightly. The rest of the girls at her table snicker and Suzie looks at them with disapproval. I hate letting my fans down, but I have a mission here on Earth and I can't forget that; ever.

Mmm, I think I'm starting to think I was a pop-star before I was D... Well you know, I don't really like saying the D word. Because I kind of like being alive, so to speak. The thing is, I love the thought of having adoring fans. Enough of my rubbish. Time to do a risk assessment; the risk being to my safety.

My eyes check around the cafeteria, I see Kurt and his followers sitting a couple of tables away from Paul. I should get a flash of purple any time. Zap, as I speak.

It's okay, don't be scared, it's only a mauve tinge and I'm becoming immune to the electrical charge.

"Hi guys, where's Jenny today?" I'm passing their table. Nowww that was no mauve tinge, that was a purrrple face, lion's fangs and all. Me thinks the little green eyed monster is at work with Kurty boy. He's trying to restrain his alter ego. It wouldn't be good for monsters to be seen in the school cafeteria and I certainly don't want to do that out of body thing on an empty stomach.

"Seems she called in sick today. I sneaked a couple of calls to her earlier, but she's not answering." Kurt sounds puzzled.

"Oh, I hope she's fine. We'll get together later, Kurt, if that's okay?" Now don't worry, that was just figurative speech. I'm not about to join up with the Red Rider and his crew.

"Sure Dan. By the way, you play some good soccer. I'll need to watch out." Purrrple face, purple face, me thinks he's finding it difficult to praise my soccer talent.

"Thanks, but I'm not up to your standard." Okay sometimes I need to lie a little, otherwise I wouldn't be a believable human. Now would I?

"Thanks Dan." He's so friendly. I jest. Yuck. Did you notice I fibbed twice to Kurty. Well if you didn't you're speed reading and you missed it. My other little fib was when I asked about Jenny. I knew Jenny wasn't at school. How did I know? Eh, a little bird told me. Okay, I read it in my in-box.

I need to put my romantic notions about Jenny to the back of my mind. I'm finding that a bit tricky. Romance isn't an option, therefore I can't allow my feelings to blur my goal. Sorry about the use of soccer terminology, again. One of my goals, there I go again, Paul, is sitting, feeding his face right now. I sit down opposite him, he looks up from his plate.

"Hey Dan, did you speak with JoJo at the counter?" he says with his mouth crammed full. I can only just make out his words.

"Hi Paul. No, why?"

"Well I was telling her about us going to Scottsdale Pavilions with Isais on Saturday, and she's offered to make us a packed lunch to take along. It seems that some of the best places to eat are real busy. She said that we shouldn't waste our day looking for a decent place when she can fix us up." Poor, gullible Paul. I smell a rat, or is it the sweet aroma of a demon? Answers by email, if you know the answer, because my Goddle is still drawing a blank. But I've come to my own conclusion and I don't think it's rat.

Chapter Thirteen

In a dream, in a vision of the night, when deep sleep falls on men as they slumber in their beds, he may speak in their ears and terrify them with warnings.

Job 33:15, 16

Demonlet Story

Kurt, Robbie, and the two new recruits are in Kurt's bedroom. Incense, and candles burn around the room. Black metal music plays loudly on Kurt's media player. Transformation into the strange purple slaves of the Red Rider has already taken place. The tails of the fantastical beings sweep forward and frothy spittle drips from their mouths.

"Satan, Satan, we applaud thee. Satan, Satan, we are your servants. Satan, Satan, assist us in delivering the righteous to your feet for destruction." The group raspingly recite, standing in front of the mirror.

The Red Rider appears in front of the four young men, his seven heads come out of the mirror one at a time causing his supporters to stumble backwards. They clumsily bump into one another, and in turn the group fall over with a thump.

"Your path in the destruction of others is being hindered by the servant of God. You must encourage him to join you, temptation must be put in his way, then his salvation will be lost forever, and he will burn in hell." The dragon spits fire as his mouths open to deliver his instructions. "Continue with your night terrors on the two sacrifices I have asked for, they can be mine. But my challenge to you, is that you recruit the pupil of the Holy One. Then and only then, will you be on your way to sit by my side." The dragon disappears suddenly without warning, and the four teenagers change back into their human form.

"What the ...?" Kurt's mother bursts into the room, but she is rendered lost for words when she sees her son and his friends standing naked before her.

§ § §

I am absolutely full of food. Aunt Sylvia made beef and potato pie for dinner, it was fantastic. She said that an English lady gave her the recipe some time back and she had always wanted to try it out. Of course, she now has the perfect guinea pig in residence.

I didn't have the bottle to ask her if the lady was another angel, or if she got the recipe when she was a human being. I suppose it doesn't really matter when she got it, I enjoyed it immensely.

I'm so stuffed I really just want to lie down. But an angelet has work to do. I don't know if you'll be surprised by where I am located, right at this moment, or not.

I'm standing on the doorstep of...? I bet you said Kurt's house. Wrooong. I'm at Jenny's. Now, no oohing and ahhing, remember I'm here to help, nothing else, and I mean, nada mas. My God I speak great Spanish as well.

Ding dong, ding dong. That's me pressing the doorbell. I can hear a dog yapping from somewhere in the house.

"Hi, can I help you?" A very attractive lady has appeared in the doorway. Wah-wee, I can see where Jenny gets her looks from. Sorry, God. Gulp. Trying not to imitate heterosexual seventeen-year-old boys with racing hormones, whose mouths would drop open, looking as though they were catching flies, when they admire a woman.

"Hi, my name's Dan Pierce. I'm a friend of Jenny's from school. I just thought that I'd pop by and see how she was. Emm, because she wasn't in school today." I discreetly wipe the saliva from the side of my mouth. Drooling isn't attractive.

"Well Dan, that's so nice. I'll go ask if she feels well enough to see you. Come in and sit in the parlor." She opens the door screen and I offer my hand to shake. I think she's slightly surprised by my impeccable manners. But you know me by now, I have an ulterior motive for touching her hand.

Stepping into the hall I quickly look round. I don't want any surprises. The last thing I want is a yapping dog nipping my heels. It looks like a nice home. An abundance of soft furnishings make it look cozy and comfortable. Gabriella isn't a comfy kind of mom, but her home certainly is. Okay, okay I know her name because I have insider info, remember. Anyway she's named after one of the most famous angels, ever. Hopefully you've read about my hero, and if you haven't you should be ashamed. Actually I just read up on him in Godipedia the other day.

I'm loitering at the parlor entrance and I'm watching Gabriella's hips wiggle down the hall towards the stairs. Sorry God. I meant to say, I'm watching Gabriella walk down the hall. I'm paying no attention to her wiggle at all.

"Dan, come up. Jenny will see you." Whilst I've been thinking of wiggling, Gabriella has climbed the stairs and she now calls from above. Above meaning, from upstairs, not heaven. My goodness, pay attention.

I climb the stairs two at a time and reach Gabriella who is standing on the top landing. She opens the door beside her and I see Jenny sitting on top of her bed. She's dressed in one of those nightgown wrap things. Okay, I don't know the proper name of what she's wearing, I'm a guy.

"Dan, what a nice surprise. Come in, you can go now Mom," says a smiling Jenny. Her skin is glowing, she doesn't look ill to me. Gabriella closes the bedroom door. "Sit down, sit down. It's great to see you." Jenny points to the chair beside her bed.

I sit down on the wicker seat. I imagine her bedroom looks like a lot of other teenage girl's rooms. Decorated in various shades of pink, fluffy fur cushions strewn across the bed, and wall shelves jammed packed with cuddly toys of all shapes and sizes. Note I say I imagine, after all I don't make a habit of visiting girl's bedrooms.

"How you feeling?" I'm using a concerned tone.

"I'm feeling a bit better than I did first thing this morning."

"Do you want to tell me what's up?"

"There's nothing up Dan, just had tummy pains. I hope I don't need to spell it out." She's gone all girly and embarrassed.

"No you don't need to spell it out. But don't kid a kidder, Jen. I just want to help you."

"Dan, you are helping, just by being here." She's acting kind of slushy now. I think she needs a bit of persuasion to tell me what's going on. I touch her hand. Oh, oh, the emotions that I'm experiencing right now are not angel like. My pulse is racing, my palms are clammy, my mouth is dry and there are strange tingling feelings in parts of my body I don't want to even acknowledge. Recognize those feelings?

I recognize them as being danger. A guy looking for his salvation must squash those feelings. Inhale, exhale, inhale, exhale.

"What's really wrong?" I'm in control.

"Sit beside me Dan; put your arm around me." She's doing that girly, flutter the eye thing. Oh God, what are you doing to me? I'm in control, I'm in control. I slide onto the bed beside her and slip my arm round her. She puts her head on my chest, her hair smells of coconut. I can feel her body tremble. I'm hoping she doesn't notice that I'm trembling too. I tighten my hold on her and she snuggles further into me.

"I'm having awful nightmares Dan. I don't really want to go into details but these purple monsters, with hands like scorpions, are coming to me in the night and... Well they're terrorizing me in my dreams. Although the monsters bear no resemblance to anything human. I know it's Kurt and his friends." She sounds so helpless.

We already know that Kurt is no longer a human, as we know it. Therefore, I need no convincing to go to her aid. Oh heck, she's crying. I begin to stroke her chin. I kiss the top of her head. Why did I do that? She's now looking up at me with tear filled, doe like eyes. She pushes herself up the bed, raises her head towards mine, and her lips are beckoning me. Tingle, tingle. I kiss her gently, her lips taste so sweet. I pull her into me, whoa boy. What am I doing? I move away from her quickly.

"Sorry Jenny, I shouldn't have done that. I betrayed our friendship." What was I thinking? Okay you don't need to spell it out.

"If you're worried about Kurt, he'll never know. It will be our secret. Dan, kissing you has made me feel a whole lot better. Better than I've felt in a long time." I hate to admit it, but she's putting her point across very persuasively. This is too dangerous; I could blow everything I want to achieve for the sake of a kiss.

"Jenny, I just want to be your friend." Did I sound convincing?

"Dan, I'm sorry I've made a terrible fool of myself." Jenny turns her head away from me.

"No you haven't; I'm to blame. You're just feeling a little vulnerable right now and I took advantage," I say apologetically. I take hold of her chin and gently turn her face back towards me. We look into each other's eyes for a moment. She sighs, slides back down the bed and snuggles into my chest again.

"You're an angel. Okay we're friends. We'll be friends forever," she says resolutely.

"Forever." I do hope we'll be friends forever. I stroke her arm; her breathing is heavy. She's fallen asleep. I stroke her hair and brush my lips across the top of her head.

"Sweet dreams my love. Sweet dreams," I whisper. What I did a moment ago was wrong because I know how she feels about me. If I get romantically involved with her, she could be in more danger than she already is.

Chapter Fourteen

Do not be far from me, for trouble is near.

Psalm 22:11

Jenny's Story

Gabriella was impressed by the young man who came to visit her daughter the previous evening. There was something special about him. He was different from Kurt, who she knew was nothing but bad news. However, Jenny wouldn't listen to anything she had to say.

So she had decided to keep her opinion of Kurt to herself. She was in no doubt that if she had aired her view of him, her view being that he was a creep, war would break out between them. Their mother-daughter relationship was too fragile to tell the truth. It was better to hope that maybe someday Jenny would think along the same lines, and dump him.

At least Jenny was looking, and feeling better today. She was up and about, and going into school. Gabriella had told her to take another day's rest, but Jenny insisted she was going in. She wondered if her keenness had anything to do with Dan. Jenny is sitting in silence eating her breakfast, and reading a teen magazine.

"You haven't mentioned Dan before, any reason?" asks Gabriella.

"No reason." Jenny's cheeks turn pink.

"He seems a nice guy and good-looking." Gabriella can see her words are having some effect on her daughter.

"Yes he is, a very nice guy. I don't know about the good-looking part." Jenny's face is now bright crimson.

"Is he a friend of Kurt's?"

"I wouldn't say a friend. Kurt doesn't really have friends, he has acquaintances." She pauses for a moment. "Mom, I would rather you didn't mention Dan coming here. To Kurt that is, I don't want you bringing the subject of Dan up at all when Kurt's around."

"Just as I thought, you've got the hots for this guy, haven't you?" teases Gabriella.

"I certainly do not. Dan is just a friend. Anyway Suzie is the one that has the hots for him," says Jenny indignantly.

"So why would you not want me to mention him to Kurt? Does Dan have a crush on you, is that it?"

"No, you're so wrong. I don't even know if Dan likes girls."

"I see. What does Kurt think of him then?"

"I don't really know. You see, Dan's new to the school, and it turns out he's an ace soccer player. I think Kurt might see him as a threat, and I wouldn't want to rub his nose in it."

"So you think there may be a bit of rivalry between the boys?" Gabriella continues to probe.

"Yeah, that's it, soccer rivalry." Jenny wishes her mom would just shut up. What's with all these questions? She swallows the last spoonful of her breakfast cereal. It was time to leave. Jenny isn't sure if her story sounds convincing, but it's what she's sticking to..

Gabriella watches her daughter leave. She suspects that the jealousy and rivalry between the boys isn't about soccer, but as to who was about to capture her daughter's heart.

§ § §

That was a close call last night at Jenny's, but I'm proud of myself. I didn't fall completely victim to temptation. I have to constantly remind myself that I am not a human being, I am a spiritual being. But when you're faced with a gorgeous young woman, it's easy to forget.

I had to come clean to Aunt Sylvia about everything.

Well, nearly everything. I was sure she would be horrified, but of course, she took it in her stride. I'm positive she knew every detail before I confessed, because as you know she has her spies.

The good news is I had reacted in a proper manner for an angelet. Hopefully they didn't spot that I enjoyed every minute of Jenny snuggling into my chest, just being near her and the kiss. Oh God, the kissss. Did you hear that? I'm doing that risky daydream thing again. A sheer fantasy that can never be realized.

Talking of fantasies, here comes Suzie and she's approaching fast. I'm aware it sounds arrogant when I say that I'm the guy she daydreams about, but it's the truth and she's one persistent old girl. I'm smiling of course, because we angelets can't be rude.

"Dan, I've been looking all over for you," says Suzie impatiently.

"What's up Suzie?" I can hardly tell her that I've been doing my utmost since I got to school this morning to avoid her.

"There's nothing up Dan, I just want to tell you the fantastic news, or do you know already?" She's calmed down a bit.

"No Suzie, I don't know the fantastic news, enlighten me."

"You and I have been picked for the roles of Frederic Henry and Catherine Barkley in the school production of 'A Farewell to Arms'. Isn't that great?" she gushingly says.

"Cool Suzie, cool." I hope Suzie didn't notice my jaw drop when I just heard that news.

"It's such a romantic story, don't you think?"

"It does have its moments." Oh, God this means I'll need to kiss Suzie. What if I enjoy that too?

"Jen, wait till you hear our news," calls out Suzie. Since she's looking behind me, I can only assume that the footsteps I hear belong to Jen. I turn around and see gooorgeous Jenny.

"I heard on my way here. All the girls are talking about you two. Congratulations." Jenny's all smiles. My heart has just missed a beat at the sound of her voice. My, my; today is already beginning to be a challenging one.

"Nothing's confirmed yet. I haven't said I'll take the part." I'm not fibbing this time.

"What are you, some kind of Hollywood actor? Dan, you auditioned for it." Jenny starts to laugh.

"I know, but surely I've got a choice whether I want to star in it or not?" I look from one girl to the other. Suzie's looking kind of panic-stricken and for once at a loss for words. She looks to her BFF for support.

"Yes you have a choice, but I've never known anyone to turn down a lead role, it's a great honor. I think you're being ridiculous Dan, you've no reason to turn it down," says Jenny.

She's trying to coax me into doing this through loyalty to her friend, but I don't think she really wants to see me kissing Suzie. Then again, maybe she was just vulnerable last night and I misread the signs. I must have misunderstood the download too. Duh, don't think so. Guys, how am I going to get out of this one? You know the script by now. Answers by email.

"Dan, don't you like me, is that it?" Suzie's annoyed with me, I can tell.

"Now who's being ridiculous Suzie. Of course I like you. It's… maybe just a bit of stage fright. That's it, stage fright." Sorry for the fibs Lord.

"Oh Dan, there's nothing to be scared of. I'll be there to hold your hand every step of the way." Warning alert, warning alert. Suzie's putting her arm round me and hugging me. Oh Suzie, I so don't want to let you down.

§ § §

Paul's sitting at our usual table in the cafeteria and his head's buried in a book.

"Hi Paul, where you been hiding out all day?" I can't wait to tell him my bit of fantastic news. I jest. He looks up from his book. Excuse me if I don't speak, it's because I'm dumbfounded. I was given no warning of this; his face is a mess. The bruises are nearly as purple as those demon guys' complexions. Okay I've recovered. "What happened to you? And don't tell me you had an accident," I say, solemnly.

"I don't know what happened." Paul sounds confused.

"Have you got some kind of amnesia?"

"I think it was Pop," says Paul. As if this kid's not got enough on his plate with the Red Rider's followers.

"Does your dad do this to you on a regular basis?"

"Yes, he does. I mentioned to you before about him drinking. He drinks too much, then beats me up for the slightest reason." Wow, he blurted that out.

"Paul he has no reason to do this to you at anytime, and I mean anytime. Have you spoken to anyone about this?"

"No, and I'm not going to. Pop's been through a lot." He's now trying to make excuses for the guy. Typical.

"There's no excuse for this; we need to get him help and you help."

"Dan, you're trying to do the right thing, but it would just make things worse."

"Trust me Paul. I'm an a… a friend." Heck I nearly said the A word. "Okay, but we're going to have to work through this together."

"Dan, you can't help me. I'll be all right." He's putting a brave face on.

"Paul, we can discuss this later. You're staying at my place tonight. You can tell your pop that you're having a sleep over. Because we're going to Scottsdale Pavilions tomorrow and we're making a day of it." I hate this fibbing thing, but on this occasion, I think it's warranted.

"Dan, you don't know what he's like. He'll be sitting in some bar and he expects me to be sitting at home, reading one book or another." Paul's pouring his little heart out. I want to hug the big guy.

"Listen, I'll get Aunt Sylvia to contact him, she'll sort it out. I'll text her right now." I need her help on this one. His dad isn't going to listen to me. In his eyes, I'm just some stupid kid.

"I'd appreciate if she could do that." He looks relieved.

"Paul, you're amongst friends." I want to tell him it's all going to be put right, but I'm not sure if it will be or not. I'll do my best though.

"Oh I don't know about that, here comes Kurt Hills." Even the bruises on Paul's face have drained of color.

Heck, no time to text Aunty. I look along the aisle and yes, the purple monsters are drawing nearer. Notice I say purple monsters, because both guys are looking kind of purply ugly. Woah, it's out of body time. Oh, my cell phone's vibrating in my pocket. I'm back into my physical form. I read the text, Sylvia's answered my request about Paul, without me even texting her. So that's taken care of.

Whoosh, out of body again. Nowhere for me to hide, the Devil's disciples have sussed me out. Hold the pastrami, it's time to, eh...shadow box. I'm calling it that, because hey, I'm now a shadow of my former self. Corny I know. Woah, I've just been grasped by a pincer. I've managed to wriggle free from Kurt's hold, as I've dispersed my molecules. The gruesome twosome is now struggling to catch sight of me. I capture them with one of my extended arms. One, two, three, I've pushed Robbie hard onto a table. One, two, three, wham, I've punched Kurty boy and he's landed on top of his BFF.

Laughing fills the cafeteria, the other students now see Kurt lying on top of Robbie on one of the tables. They're in a rather compromising position. Their faces are close, and I mean really close together. They look like they're having a little smooch, and macho guys like these don't smooch. Especially with each other, well, not in public anyway.

I told you I was having one of those challenging days, but it seems not as challenging as the two demonlets are having, that's for certain.

Chapter Fifteen

I broke the fangs of the wicked and snatched the victims from their teeth.

Job 29:17

Paul stayed over as planned last night, with no opposition from his father. Isais obligingly took Aunt Sylvia and I over to pick Paul up. Isais was so shocked when he saw Paul's injuries that he wanted to go have a word with George, but we managed to talk him out of it. Well, we didn't actually talk him out of it. Aunt Sylvia touched his arm and defused what could have been potentially a very nasty situation with her angel powers.

Paul managed to put all his troubles behind him when all four of us went over to Scottsdale Pavilions. On Friday nights, local musicians gather together and put on free concerts. The group who were performing last evening were doing a jam session. No rehearsing, no sheets of music, nada. They were just getting on down, awesome. We had a superb time.

If you ever go over there, you should go see what's on. Check out the website for details, that's what Isais does all the time. Of course no night would be classed as awesome if you didn't finish with foood. After the concert, we went to a real cool diner. I had a cheeseburger with bacon, French fries, and of course the compulsory strawberry milkshake. A growing boy like me needs all the calories he can eat. Paul and Isais on the other hand could do without the calories, but they went ahead and consumed lots. Too much to even bore you with the details.

Did you notice that the circumstances of how Paul came about his injuries hadn't been downloaded to us.

That makes me think that it wasn't his pop that did the damage. I have my suspicions as to who the culprit, or culprits, were. My suspicions being of a purple hue. Because when I tried to access Paul's history my tablet kept crashing, and Aunt Sylvia's did as well. Could be a devil in the works.

No more time for this chat. Got to get on with some things right now. We'll catch up later. "!Hasta luego!" There's that Spanish thing again. "See you later."

§ § §

Jenny's Story

"I was disappointed in Dan's reaction yesterday, about the play," complains Suzie over the phone.

Jenny is lying on top of her bed. She has been listening to Suzie moan for the last ten minutes, non-stop. She doesn't understand what Suzie's problem is; Dan is doing the play now, end of story.

Her mind drifts, she thinks of Dan. She had wanted him to keep kissing her the other night. She wanted it so much. She imagines his face next to hers. She closes her eyes. She feels his presence, she smells his aftershave. She feels his lips gently glance across her hair, her forehead, her cheek, the tip of her nose, and her lips. Their lips never actually uniting. She can feel the passion between them.

"Jenny, are you still there?" Suzie's voice intrudes her dream moment with Dan.

"Oh, yes, Suzie, I am. Go on, I'm listening." She twiddles with the ends of her long blonde hair.

"I don't think you were," says Suzie firmly.

"Suzie, go on." Jenny's so, so bored. She lifts her leg up and looks at her painted toenails. The color's called 'Devil Red'. It was a present from Kurt.

The voile curtains suddenly float into the room and the

window thumps shut. Jenny jumps involuntarily. She sits up and looks around her room, it's as though someone was with her. Lying back down, she relaxes again, but her mind isn't on the call. Her mind's on Dan. Jenny knows that it's impossible for Dan to have actually been there with her, but just for a millisecond she felt he could have been.

§ § §

We're at the car show, we had lunch hours ago. Now I bet that surprised you. We ate at a place that was highly recommended by Isais. It seems Ashkii enjoyed the food there. I had a huge filled flat bread. Mmm, mmm. Stu-pen-dous. And the iced limeade was just the thing for a hot day like today. Re-fresh-ing. Ashkii had good taste. Poor kid, I don't know much about him; other than Isais seems to miss him lots.

As it's now just after five, and we had munchies at two, there's still time to partake a burger or two later on. But let's forget my stomach for a while, because I need to tell you about some of these fantastic classic automobiles that I'm surrounded by.

The cars range from Hot Rods to Muscle Cars. In this line alone there's a Pontiac GTO, a Plymouth Road Runner, a Deuce coupe, and a T-Bucket. Awesome. I'm in heaven. Well, not really, I don't think cars go to the big place in the sky. Then again, maybe they do. I'll tell you when I get there. I here you say, not when, but if, I get there. I'm thinking along those lines myself at present.

Paul and Isais are really hitting it off. It's a pity Paul's pop isn't like Isais. But Aunt Sylvia's working on George. She's told me to leave that to her. So who am I to disagree with my elders?

What could spoil this perfect day? Got it in one; a demon. Although I can't confirm she is one, I have my suspicions. Here comes JoJo!!

"Hi boys and Isais, I've been looking everywhere for

you. I've got plenty of food to share over in my car. Dan, if you want to come over with me and get it," says JoJo pushily. I hesitate, I'm not too keen on going anywhere with JoJo. Heck, my brain's working overtime. God, I could be doing with some help here.

"Thanks for the offer JoJo, but we've already eaten and we have plans for later," says Isais. Could that be the help I asked for? Oh, oh. She didn't like that reply. I'm now seeing JoJo in a different light. She's changing from that big jovial woman that I told you about into a very strange red creature with a serpent's head and tongue. Her tongue's wriggling rapidly in and out of her mouth. It's no wonder I couldn't Goddle her. Body swerve, swerve. That big pointy tongue keeps forking in my direction. Ooh, ah, it just missed me.

"I'm disappointed in you, Paul. I told you to tell Dan that I was bringing a picnic for you boys." She's acting as though she's sensitive. Why is she picking on Paul? Paul's head drops in embarrassment.

"It was very kind of you JoJo, but it wasn't Paul, or Dan's, decision to turn down your offer, it was mine. So if you don't mind, us boys are going to get on with our day," says Isais assertively. Good job Isais and Paul can't see her tongue, because it's whipping over their heads like a quirt. "Come on boys, I want to look at that 1999 Ford Cobra up here." Isais walks away. Duck, duck. No not as in waterfowl, I mean bend over, dip, I have to get out of her way.

The three of us are walking away from her now and she isn't pleased. How do I know that? I think it's the head spinning that's the give away, and I don't mean she's suffering from an attack of dizziness.

I glance behind; phew, she can't lash out at us with her tongue any longer, we're too far away from her.

"Are you okay Dan?" asks Paul.

"I'm great, why are you asking?"

"You were acting real strange back there. You were hopping about, while we were speaking with JoJo. I know she isn't happy with us, because her face looked like it was about to burst. But you aren't scared of her, are you?"

"Oh yeah, the hopping thing. It's got nothing to do with JoJo, I need to go to the restroom. I think I must have drank too much iced limeade earlier, emphasis being on the too much ice."

"Forget JoJo boys. Dan you go to the restroom, Paul and I will be looking at the Cobra. We'll meet you there," says Isais enthusiastically.

"She was mad though, wasn't she? At one point I imagined her tongue was wriggling about," says Paul, laughing.

"You thought her tongue was wriggling. Huh, you're crazy buddy. I'll catch up with you at the Cobra. Wriggling indeed, I think you've had too much sun." I force a laugh.

I leave my two friends, I think I will go to the restroom, and splash my face with cold water, or something. I'm not going to explain what the something is. Use your imagination.

Hey, before I leave you; I want to speak about JoJo. It seems I was right to suspect her after all. What I can't work out, is how Isais knows her. Remind me to try and find out. Now give a guy some privacy to go do whatever he has to do in the restroom.

Chapter Sixteen

Show me the way I should go.

Psalm 143:8

Buzz, buzz, buzz. No it's not my earring making that sound, it's the school bell ringing for end of lesson.

"Right folks, that's all the time we have for today. Dan and Suzie, that was good, but not great. Dan, I need you to be a bit more enthusiastic. Frederic Henry isn't the shy and retiring type. And I know you certainly aren't.

"Put more of yourself into it. Give it a bit more pizzazz. Suzie, well done, I think you've captured Catherine Barkley perfectly." Miss Summerville's eyes search around the classroom and she continues in her authoritarian manner, "Paul Mitchum and Jenny Green, please stay behind for a moment. Rest of the class read over the next scene and for any of you who don't have parts as yet, and would really like one, I suggest you practice, practice."

Suzie's face is flushed with excitement, she's been stuck to my side like glue for the last couple of hours. Now laughter is circulating around the classroom, they're laughing for no good reason other than it's the end of class.

"Yes, Miss Summerville," say the drama group all together.

My drama teacher doesn't know the dread that fills me as she critiques my debut performance. This guy Hemingway's words are enough to make any teenage guy blush. Then there's the small matter of Suzie and I kissing. Yes I said kissing. For the sake of the play, only. It's a problem. The fact that I enjoyed it is the problem.

If I was a hot bloodied heterosexual male I'd be looking forward to our scenes together. But as you know, my body temperature is a tad on the cold side.

I know, I know, you think I'm performing all the time as Dan Pierce. But how do we know that I'm not actually Dan Pierce? What you're seeing, or in your case, reading, could be the real McCoy. Well a manifestation of the real one. I can hear my name being called, I better listen.

"Dan, focus on Hemingway's words, absorb them. Frederic Henry is a passionate man and he desires Catherine. I chose you, Dan, for the lead because you have an unexplainable stage presence. So don't let me down." Miss Summerville is making me feel kind of guilty. I think it's time to knuckle down. She's right though, I do have a certain charisma, but we all know why that is.

"I won't disappoint you Miss Summerville."

"I hope not Dan." She's frowning at me over the top of her spectacles.

§ § §

I'm sitting looking into my cold chicken salad, which so far isn't making my mouth water. Paul hasn't arrived, as yet, from drama class. He's going to be knocked out with the news that he's been chosen for the part of the Lieutenant Rinaldi, Henry's roommate, in the play. As will Jenny be, with her role as Helen Ferguson. The news isn't official yet, but I have some insider information.

I'm looking over at the serving area of the cafeteria, and I can see Kurt and JoJo in deep conversation across the serving tray of French fries. It isn't an informal talk, because both have changed into their devilish persona.

It looks quite strange to see a long tongued serpent serving a purple faced monster with French fried potatoes. But hey, nothing shocks me anymore. C'est la vie, well that's an angelet's life anyway. I hope you're impressed at my new French linguistic skills. It must be all those fries I'm eating.

I've been thinking quite a bit, since my arrival in Scottsdale. I have so many questions that I would like answered. Who am I really? How did I die? Am I a bad guy? Am I an American? Was I born in Scottsdale, or did I die here? It crossed my mind that I could be Isais' son, but instinct tells me I'm not.

The only other human I've been made aware of, who has died in the last year or two, is Paul's mom. I'm hoping I wasn't a woman. No offense intended to my adoring female fans. Ha, ha.

The demon and Kurt are still cozy on the other side of the room. His fries must be cold by now. JoJo; how does Isais know her? His frosty reception to her on Saturday gave me the impression that there was no love lost between them. I wish Aunt Sylvia would answer some of my questions, but so far she's keeping her answers to the bare minimum. I tried Goddling Isais, but nothing much comes up. Just the usual stuff like age, place of birth, so on, so on.

I mentioned just now about Paul's mom being dead and I'd like you to keep that to yourself at present, because Paul hasn't got around to telling me. I'm sure he will in his own time.

What's happening with us today? This little tête-à-tête we're having is getting a bit serious; we need to liven up a little. You know I don't really like doing serious. Life's too short. Ha, ha.

One last thing I want to say to you before Paul arrives is that I'm really glad you've stuck around, I need close buddies like you right now. I know I'm being soppy, but it comes from the heart, kid.

Here's Paul; at last. You should see his face, he looks so happy. In fact, he looks ecstatic.

"Well kiddo, what you looking so pleased about?" Sorry about the fib.

"Dan, I've got a part in the play. I'm playing Rinaldi. Can you believe it?"

"That's great, I never saw that coming. So, has Jenny got a part too?" I swallow hard.

"Yes, she's Suzie's understudy."

Well quelle surprise, my information was wrong. How did that happen? I hope no one devil like has been intercepting my mail.

"That's wonderful news," I say sincerely. Heck, I hope Suzie doesn't take ill, because I can't kiss Jenny again, that would be bad, bad news. Oh God, please look after Suzie.

"I fancy celebrating, how about we ask Isais if he wants to go out for a pizza with us tonight?" Paul's exhilarated.

"Yes we could do that. You really get on well with Isais don't you?"

"Yes he's a real cool guy. I always feel safe when he's around."

"That's good; I feel the same way about him." I think maybe I should wish that Isais was here right now, because on my devdar, I can see purple monsters on the horizon. Devdar being the same as radar but for dev…

Whoosh, whoosh! You're wondering what the noise is? Well that was Kurt's telson whizzing past my head. Don't worry, I've transformed into my form that's more apt for fighting the devil's accomplices.

Whoop! That's me jumping over his head. Holy Moses, never knew I could jump that high. I'm having to spread my particles about. OMG, that tail of his is swinging all over the place.

"Crrrut, crrrut, crrrut." He's making a horrible rasping sound. He's never done that before. Do you hear it? I don't think it will be long before he has full demon powers.

I think I need to touch him in some way. My heavenly powers should weaken his strength. I read that last night, in the trouble-shooting part of my heavenly app. *Whoosh, whoosh.* You got it in one, it's the tail again. Why is he so angry with me? It's not my fault his French fries are cold. He's opening that big mouth of his, look at those fangs. I bet you're glad you can't see them.

"My, my, what big teeth you have." Somehow I don't think he's going to say, All the better to eat you with. Because he's not the wolf in 'Little Red Riding Hood', is he?

"It doesn't need to be like this, angel. You still have time to join us. Help us destroy the good. The Red Rider will reward you," he gurgles.

"I don't plan to swim in the Lake of Fire; ever. You don't understand Kurt, evil will never win. The Devil himself knows that first hand, he was expelled from heaven because of his rebellious antics. You should put your boss's name in a search engine, gather up some facts. If you don't have the keyboard skills, try reading John Milton's, 'Paradise Lost'. Or a good place to start would be a Holy book of some sort. He features in most."

His pincers are clicking. I suspect he's going to try to pinch me in some way. Here it comes. I feel force surge through my body. White light flows from my arm, from my whole spiritual body. I grab hold of his pincer. I'm gritting my teeth. He's one tough cookie. Thud. He drops to the ground. I slip back into my human body.

"Kurt, did you enjoy your trip?" someone shouts.

I have to stifle my amusement as Kurt lies on the floor of the cafeteria, his French fries scattered all over the place. But best of all, a plate of custard is sitting on top of his head. The thick yellow liquid drips down his face.

Roars of laughter are emanating from all over the hall.

"What the heck happened to Kurt?" Paul's baffled.

"I didn't notice, he must have stumbled or something." I think I'll tuck into my salad now, before I have to tell any more little white lies. I'm famished.

Chapter Seventeen

I have strayed like a lost sheep. Seek your servant.

Psalm 119:176

Paul and I are playing air guitar, bending backwards and forwards, we've got all the maneuvers down to a T. Paul came over just after school and I've been teaching him the finer qualities of Rock Music. We started at A, being a fantastic place to start. There're some fantastic bands in this world.

"Has anyone ever told you, Dan, that you're crazy?" Paul's eyes are sparkling with excitement.

"All the time, my big buddy, all the time." I'm busting a gut to help him start enjoying life. Bullies are hard enough to cope with, but when the Devil is stirring the pot, it's not something that can be fixed by speaking to a parent, teacher, or guardian, is it?

Whoa, Paul's now playing air guitar on his back. Ah, ah, ah, I'm now rolling on the floor laughing at his antics. I think I just heard the door bell, but no worries because Aunt Sylvia will answer it.

Is that footsteps coming along the hallway? Heck, I can't hear above the noise of my music. If it's someone for me they'll come on in, I'm sure. I've rejoined Paul and I'm plucking my air guitar with fervor. You should see me, I have some great moves. Wiggling my hips, throwing my hair back. Well, maybe not the latter, because as you know I don't have any locks to throw about.

The door opens and Aunt Sylvia pops her head in. "Dan, I sent Jenny on through to see you. But she's just disappeared out the front door," she says loudly. I stop in my tracks. Paul winks at me and he carries on playing his fictitious instrument. Aunt Sylvia steps aside and I dash past her. I reach the front door, push open the fly screen, and run out onto the front porch. I can see Jenny walking quickly up the street, in fact, she's trotting.

"Jenny," I shout, but she doesn't look back. I'll need to go after her. In superhero style I leap off the porch onto the pathway, jumping over the three steps down. I'm now onto the sidewalk, following Jenny.

"Hey, Jenny, hold up," I shout again.

She looks back. "Dan, I'll catch you tomorrow at school. It was nothing important. I shouldn't have called round. Get back to your friends." This chick is walking at a great rate of knots. But she can't escape a little speedster like me.

"Jen, you're a friend too." I've caught up with her and I take hold of her arm. She stops suddenly, I'm looking straight into her face, she is so gorrrgeous. Why am I telling you that? You're better not knowing, then you won't be tempted to tell anyone else.

"Dan, I know I shouldn't have run off. But you and Paul sounded as though you were having so much fun, I didn't want to intrude." She smiles and I slip my arm round her shoulder. I can feel her body relax. Now, now, behave yourself.

"You're not intruding, Jenny. We're all pals together. We're going out for a pizza with Isais and you're coming along. Okay girl?" I hug her.

"Oh Dan, I'd better not. You'll be discussing, eh, guy things."

"No chance of that. The only excuse I'm accepting from you for not coming along, is that you've just eaten a four course meal. So have you?"

"No." She giggles.

"That's settled then. You're hanging around with the

coolest guys in school tonight, and of course Isais as well. He's a real cool dude for an older guy."

She giggles again and what a nice giggle it is; nice like her. I'm definitely venturing into that territory named dangerous. It's time I woke up and smelt the coffee. I'm an angelet, not a real dude. Okay, that's me telling me off. Let's go for pizza, and maybe fries, and a milkshake and…

§ § §

After much debate, we have finally decided on dining in one of the restaurants in Scottsdale Fashion Square, in East Camelback Road. It's just a short ride from Aunt Sylvia's place in Wingate. We're eating in a smart restaurant, no diner for us tonight. I was totally blown away by its entrance lobby. It has a black marble floor and the walls are lined with shiny glass cases, exhibiting some truly awesome looking desserts.

The decor in general is very grand. But you don't need to be wearing your best bib and tucker to dine here, they call it casual dining. If you could see us motley crew, you would say it's very, very casual dining indeed. I believe it's not the cheapest place in town, but hey, it's a celebration meal we're out for. Aunt Sylvia kindly gave me an advance on my allowance, after I groveled a bit. Because a hungry dude like me needs to make sure he has enough dinero with him. I'm speaking Spanish again, guys.

It's just after six-thirty, and the place is busy. Diners are packed in for Happy Hour. Our waitress for the evening is called Myleene. I can see by Paul's blushes that he thinks Myleene is kind of cute and I think the attraction is reciprocated. He's a handsome big guy, but short on confidence.

The four of us are seated in one of the plush velvet booths that fill the place. I'm sitting opposite Jenny, she's sooo gorg... nice.

"Right kids, have you decided on what you're having?" Isais glances around the table at us.

"Yeah," we all say together. Myleene is using a small hand-held computer to take our orders. She drops the stylus, and it bounces onto the table top in front of Paul. I've never seen him move so quickly. He picks the pen like object up and places it back into the waitress's hand. His hand hesitates in hers, for just a brief second, but probably long enough to feel something that resembles an electric shock, through his body.

Not that I would know the feeling. I've just heard about the sensation that tingles through my body. Sorry, not my body, but a human's body when they find a certain individual absolutely gorgeous. Eh, let's talk about them, not me. Okay, you should see them, they just can't take their eyes off each other. Way to go, Paul.

Talking of electric shock waves, Jenny kicks me under the table and smiles as she tips her head towards the two love birds. I can't help but notice a starry like twinkle in Jenny's eyes as she holds her gaze on me. OMG, there I go again.

"Well kids, what're we waiting for? Dan, tell the girl what you're wanting," Isais says eagerly.

"Pizza with a Thai chicken topping and molten chocolate cake to follow," I say rapidly.

"Adriatic chicken salad, for me and fresh strawberry shortcake, please," says Jenny.

"Deluxe burger and em, cupcake for me," Paul says dreamily. Jenny giggles at Paul's lovestruck behavior and Isais shakes his head in disbelief.

"As no one seems to have ordered an appetizer, I'll order one for all of us. We'll have an assortment appetizer platter to share, and make it a big one. For my main, I'll have Spanish pot-roast, with warm sticky caramel bread pudding for dessert. Thanks. Oh, and four regular colas." Isais's making sure we don't go hungry or thirsty.

"Thanks folks." Myleene smiles to each of us as she removes our menus. She's keeping the best till last: Paul. Way to go buddy. She gives him a coy smile. Paul sighs loudly, the rest of us can't hold in our laughter at his preoccupied behavior. Isais, Jenny, and I laugh so loudly that some of the other diners look at us in bewilderment. We're going to have a good time tonight, I can feel it. I can feel it tingling through my body.

§ § §

Isais stops the truck in front of Paul's house. Jenny, who has been sitting alone in the rear seat, opens the door beside her and leaps out unexpectedly.

"Thanks for the ride Isais, but I'm okay from here. Thanks for letting me tag along boys. I'll catch up with you guys tomorrow," says Jenny. She's started to walk hurriedly away and I haven't even managed to clamber out of the truck yet because I'm jammed in front, between Paul and Isais. The word sandwiched would probably describe my situation better. I'm the sandwich filling and they're the two chunky slices of bread, either side. Paul finally gets out onto the sidewalk and I scramble out.

"Jenny, wait a minute. I'll walk you home," I shout after her and she stops.

"I can take her home," says Paul.

"Listen, if Kurt sees you with her, he'll beat the living daylights out of you both, so I don't think it's a good idea my big buddy," I say dissuasively to Paul. He winks, then nods in agreement.

"Well who's the lucky guy that's going to escort me home?" Jenny has walked back towards us, but she's stopped a short distance away.

"Me, Jenny, me. Goodbye guys and thanks for a great

night." I'm running along the pavement to meet up with her, but she's started to walk on once again. Heck, I know girls like the guy to do the chasing, but this is ridiculous. Health warning, I wouldn't recommend running after consuming a pizza and chocolate cake.

§ § §

The walk to Jenny's place has taken no time at all. We've arrived at her gate; the semi-detached house is in darkness.

"Do you want to come in?" says Jenny awkwardly. I'm kind of hesitant about going into the house with her, especially when her mom's not home. All joking aside, it's not that I don't trust myself, because I do. Do you think it sounds arrogant when I tell you that it's Jenny I don't trust, because without a doubt she has the serious hots for me. Okay, I sound arrogant.

Sooo, will I, won't I, go into the house with her? I have to make an executive decision here, because your silence isn't helping me much. I'm in her life for a reason, I need to put all my misgivings aside.

"I promise I won't jump you, if that's what you're scared of Dan," says Jenny jokingly.

"I'm not scared, Jenny. I'm quaking in my sneakers." We both laugh and start to walk up the front path. She opens the front door and clicks on the hall light and she says,

"Where do you want to sit?"

"On a chair preferably." The joke is to masquerade the fact that my nerves are jangling.

"You're mad Dan, mad. I meant, do you want to go up to my room, or do you want to sit in the parlor?"

"Where would you prefer?" I'm acting nonchalant.

"My room. I can put on some music. I'd like if you would go over my lines for the play with me."

"Okay, cool. But won't your mom be angry if she comes home and I'm in your bedroom with you?"

"It won't be a problem, Dan. She's very liberal and she likes you. So she wouldn't mind if we were getting it on."

"But Jenny, you do know we won't be getting it on, don't you?" Please God, give a guy a break.

"I know Dan, we're just good friends." Jenny sighs. She starts to climb the stairs and I watch her slim legs and hips. She has the exact same wiggle as her mom. Watching her move so gracefully up the stairs makes me feel so alive. Whoa boy, whoa, I can't go upstairs with her. All sorts of feelings are rushing through me and none of them are angelic. No way can I follow her upstairs.

"Jenny, I'm going to go now. I think it would be for the best," I say with restraint.

She turns around suddenly, losing her footing as she does so. She starts to tumble down the stairs towards me and I spring forward to her rescue. I manage to catch her before she lands on her bottom. She grabs onto me, putting her arms tightly around my neck. An electric shock has just bounced through my body and it isn't caused by my earring.

Our faces touch, nose to nose, lips to lips. I can smell her perfume as I kiss her forcefully on the mouth. What the heck am I doing? I break our mouth contact, pulling myself away from her. "Jenny we're friends, just friends." I remove her arms from around my neck and put them down by her sides. She looks at me in bafflement. I take hold of her hands. "I'm so, so sorry Jenny. We have to say goodnight right here, please forgive me Jenny." I'm such a jerk, I don't think I'm up to this angel stuff. How am I going to explain this to Aunt Sylvia?

Chapter Eighteen

Our Father… deliver us from the evil one.

Matthew 6:9.13

Jenny's Story

"So what did you get up to last night Jenny?" Suzie had run across the main concourse to catch up with her friend, both were on their way to food science class. Jenny had been worried about this moment all morning, but it was impossible to avoid Suzie forever.

"Oh, we went out for a meal."

"Oh my, oh my, Kurt taking you out for meals now. What's he been up to?" Suzie is full of cynicism.

"I didn't go out with Kurt, he was otherwise occupied." Jenny gulps air before she continues,"I went out with Dan last night."

"On a date?" Suzie's face turns bright pink. She feels as though her friend has just kicked her hard in the stomach.

"Don't be silly. Paul Mitchum and Isais Bia, a neighbor of Dan's, were there too."

"All I want to know is how you happened to go out with Dan for dinner?" Suzie wants her friend to justify what she believes is betrayal of their friendship.

"I forgot my copy of the play and I dropped in to ask Dan if he had a spare." Jenny makes an effort to cover up her disloyalty.

"And why would you ask Dan Pierce if he had a spare copy?"

"Well, I had taken Kushi out for a walk, and as I was walking past Dan's I thought, 'Hey, Dan might have a spare

copy. I'll just go in and ask.'"

"I don't believe you Jenny Green. You never take your mom's mutt out for a walk. You always say you hate it."

"Mom and I have been getting on well lately, so I thought I'd do something for her for once in my life. I've realized that she always tries to do her best for me."

"Your new found compassion for your mother is very touching Jenny, but you're a liar. No wonder you wouldn't put in a good word for me. You've been after him yourself all this time." Suzie looks at her friend in disbelief.

"Suzie, Dan is just a friend. I wish you'd get that into your thick skull. I have a boyfriend, as you well know."

"Yes, I know. And I wonder what he'll say when he knows that you went out with Dan last night," says Suzie vindictively.

"Suzie, you know that'll just wind him up. Please believe me, there's nothing going on between Dan and I. Please don't tell Kurt." Jenny is suddenly angst-ridden.

"Jenny Green I never want to speak to you as long as I live. You've let me down. It's no way to treat a girlfriend."

"I know you feel let down, but I haven't done anything that I should be ashamed of. The guys were on their way out to the Square and they asked me to join them. That's it. No hidden agenda. Suzie, nothing's going on. Listen, we're going to be late for class, let's meet up after school and discuss this."

"You must be joking." Suzie storms off ahead. Jenny knows that her friend can be very spiteful and prays that she won't tell Kurt.

§ § §

Goooal, goooal. Don't you just love it when those Latino soccer commentators shout that on the TV. Hopefully that's what I'm going to be running around shouting in the next ninety minutes. I'm in the changing rooms getting ready for a friendly game of soccer against Liberty High School. I've heard they've got some wicked players. But I can guarantee their players won't be as wicked as some of ours. If you get my gist.

Speaking of wicked, here comes Kurt. Things between us boys are rather tense right now. I'm not playing the devil game he wants to play and he's thrown his pacifier, or is it his Lucifer, out of the baby buggy? Every time we meet up, he turns into that horrible purple guy and today is no different. You're sooo lucky that you can't see him. He's vanished round the corner but I can hear him rasping as he makes his way between the lockers.

He seems particularly upset with me today. I have to assume he knows about a certain little lady and me last night. Suzie and I met up earlier and things between her and Jen have been smoothed over. I convinced her, using my little cherub charm, that Jen and I are just good friends and she's okay with that. For now anyway. So all is rosy in the garden between the girls again. BFF.

Buzzz, buzzz, my earrings buzzing. There's a purrrple guy approaching and he's attempting to practice a soccer move called dribbling, but he's doing it all wrong.

"Hey Kurt, you're suppose to dribble with your feet not your mouth." Ha, ha. Gross; the saliva's dripping all over the floor. Panic over, the other teams have arrived and Kurty is changing back to his gorgeous self. I jest.

§ § §

Paul's sitting in drama class reading over what I recognize as the script of the play. We're both a little early for class. I like to get myself settled before the teach arrives, as does Paul.

"Big boy, what you been up to this morning?" I slap my buddy on the back and sit down beside him.

"Hi, Dan, had some free study time earlier so I've been trying to learn some of these lines."

"You'll be great, don't worry."

"Had a great time last night Dan. How did you and Jenny get on?" Paul nudges me suggestively.

"We got on fine. Walked her home, made sure she got into the house okay. Then came straight back home." I know I've kept out some important happenings, but you didn't want to read them again, did you?

"Are you not scared Kurt will come after you?"

"No, why should he?"

"Well, she's his girl, and she clearly likes you a lot. As all the girls do. I've also noticed that Kurt isn't as nice to you as he was at the onset."

"I think you're exaggerating about all the girls liking me Paul. Back to Kurt; any conflict between Kurt and I has nothing to do with Jenny, I can guarantee you that. I know Jenny likes me, but we'll never be an item."

"Why not?"

"Eh, she's not my type."

"Is Suzie your type then?"

"No, I've still to decide what my type is Paul."

"Oh, do you not like girls then? I mean if you don't, it wouldn't matter to me."

"I know, my big friend, it would make no difference to you, but the fact is I really do like them. It's just I don't have time for them at present. With my studies, soccer, and all. I need to keep focused. I've got lots of hard work ahead. Does that answer your question kiddo?"

"Okay Dan, I won't ask you anymore prying questions."

"Paul, you can ask me anything. But as to whether you'll get the answer you expect I don't really know. I've got a question for you. Who do you rock, amongst the girls?"

"Jenny, she's lovely. But Suzie is beautiful," says Paul

bashfully. My, my he's a real dark horse.

"You've been keeping that a secret, haven't you?"

"Yes, because she would never go out with me."

"I bet she would if you asked her."

"Never. It's you she likes."

"Paul, never say never."

"Listen Dan, it would be a miracle if she ever saw me in a romantic sense."

"Miracles happen my man, miracles happen." I hug my friend. The rest of the class have arrived and here comes the girls. So it's time to act like real cool dudes. I forgot, we already are. No need to play act, we'll just be our natural selves then. I heard that, you little devil.

Chapter Nineteen

Cast all your anxiety on him because he cares for you.

1 Peter 5:7

I've just finished showering; I can tell you I smell absolutely gorgeous. I'll drive the girls wild. I jest, that's the last thing I want to do. You don't need to shut your eyes, I'm decent, I've got my clothes on. I wouldn't speak to you otherwise, as I'm a modest kind of guy.

Isais lowered my ears earlier, when I came home from school. Don't be silly, Isais isn't a plastic surgeon. What I meant was; he gave me a haircut. So I'm looking very smart, according to Aunt Sylvia and Isais anyway.

I'm waiting on Paul, Jenny, and Suzie to arrive. Yes, the girls have been invited around tonight and we're going to rehearse. You may have noticed that Kurt doesn't seem to be so interested in Jenny, or Paul, any longer. The fact is, Kurt has bigger fish to fry, meaning me of course.

But don't be fooled, I believe he's still terrorizing them in some way. As long as he's one of the Red Rider's followers he'll try and cause havoc in people's lives. I think that's Isais's truck I can hear pulling up outside. He went to pick up Paul and the girls. He was also under orders to buy a tub of vanilla ice-cream to accompany one of Sylvia's famous fruit pies, which we plan to munch on later. Need to dash. We'll talk in a while.

§ § §

Demon's Story

"Satan, Satan, Satan," JoJo recites. The woman changes, in the blink of an eye, into her demon state. Her serpent shaped

head thrusts upwards. Her tongue spirals, uncontrollably. She slithers down onto the floor as her master appears in front of her. The red scales on Satan's rotating heads glisten in the lamplight. His seven mouths open and shut as he breathes fire.

"Oh master, I need your continuing strength, guidance and tolerance," says his disciple.

"You have failed me, my godless accomplice. My young supporters struggle with their tasks. I am growing tired of them. Why should I not surrender them to God's soldiers?" The Red Rider spits fire.

"Oh master, I have not failed. It would be such a waste to destroy the young enthusiastic foot soldiers in question. The young holy crusader is just proving a little more than they can manage, at this time. He is one of the best recruits Michael has enlisted in a long while. But Daniel will falter at some point. He will succumb to temptation."

"This is my world, no one else's, and those who fail me, must be destroyed."

"Do not fret. Your many foot soldiers will ensure this world belongs to you and you alone."

"You have met with a skin-walker; has he proven troublesome?"

"Do not worry about him, my powers will take care of him, if necessary."

"I hope that you will take care of him. What about the young humans? When will I be totally in possession of their souls?"

"Please, oh Satan, just give me some more time with my boys."

"I grant you more time. You are a loyal servant, but your time and my patience are running out, my wise serpent."

"Thank you, my eternal master, I will not disappoint you."

§ § §

It's been cray-zeee in here since Isais dropped the

kids off. We four amigos have been continually fooling around for the last hour. So much so, that Aunt Sylvia has just stuck her head around the door and warned us that if we don't get on with our practice, there'll be no munchies for us later. You should see Paul's face at the thought of no sweet treats. Boohoo.

"Right guys, where are we?" says my big buddy bossily.

"In Dan's bedroom," says Suzie jokingly.

"Seriously, where are we in the play?" Paul tries not to laugh at her inane comment. We need to get down to work, otherwise the girls will do nothing but flirt with us cool handsome boys all night and not a line will have been rehearsed.

"Right, pay attention. We've just finished the scene between the Priest and Frederic Henry. Henry's about to be transferred to another hospital. The two friends speak about loving God. Frederic says that he doesn't love God, but he's been afraid of him in the night." For once I'm being serious-minded.

"That's like you and your weird nightmares Jen," interrupts Suzie.

"It's not. God isn't in them; it's purple things. Suzie, don't embarrass me. Let's get on." Jenny's angry at her friend for disclosing her secrets. I can see Paul's reaction when Jen mentions purple things. He desperately wants to ask her about her dreams, but he holds back.

"Stop fooling around girls. Let's get this done, then we can chat about anything we want. But later, okay?" I say sensibly. I want desperately to talk about the dreams but now is not the time.

"We're ready to start the scene where Frederic has arrived in a hospital in Milan. He's lying in bed. He's been pining for Catherine, asking if she's around. He's really pining. Then, after hearing footsteps coming down the corridor, he sees her. His goddess. When she walks through that door, he knows instantly that he loves her. She kisses him and one thing leads to another, if you know what I mean. They pledge their love for each other. I mean, they love each other mega," says Suzie sexily.

The girls start to giggle and Paul snickers. The palms of my hands have suddenly become sweaty. The word pallid describes my face color perfectly. It's the glint in Suzie's eye that's making me nervous. Well, here I go, like a lamb to the slaughter.

§ § §

That wasn't so bad. I managed to convince everyone that we only needed to rehearse the lines, nothing else. So no kissing was required. Suzie tried not to look too upset.

We've moved through to the kitchen, where Aunt Sylvia's laid out our sweet treats. Four bowls, spoons, the apple-pie, with a chunk missing, and the ice-cream with a scoop gone await us. Accompanied by a jug of lemonade and four glasses, which I suppose are there in case we need to wash it down. But I find more ice-cream normally does the trick.

The missing food was eaten by Isais, being his payment for picking my friends up earlier. We couldn't let him go without a reward. We all sit down at the table. Paul and I sit together with the girls opposite.

"Who's going to be mother?" I ask.

"I will," volunteers Jenny. "Do you want a small piece, or a large piece, of pie, Suzie?" She's poised with my aunt's mother of pearl handled cake slicer at the ready.

"Small please." Suzie indicates the size she wants by drawing an outline on the table top with her forefinger. Jenny scores the knife across the top of the pastry. She etches out the required portion and then cuts deep down into the filling. She's struggling to take the piece out, it's sliding off the cake slice. Panic over, she's managed to lift it and she puts it into one of the awaiting bowls. Suzie lifts the bowl away from Jenny and places it in the center of the table. She slides two replacements, for Paul and I, over to her friend.

"I take it you boys will want large slices? Don't bother answering, because it was a real dumb question." Jenny slices into the pie. This time she doesn't mark out the piece size, she cuts into the pastry straight away.

"That was a stupid question Jenny, because Paul's already tried Aunt Sylvia's pies previously and he knows that they are the best ever." I look at Paul who's nodding in agreement; he can't take his eyes away from the edibles. We're drooling at the chunks of sticky apple that are falling out of the pastry case back into the pie plate. Jenny scoops them up and puts an equal amount of the wayward contents on top of each of the large slices that are now in the two bowls.

Jenny plops a scoop of ice-cream into one of the dessert bowls and slides it across the table to Paul, he immediately tucks in. Jenny serves ice-cream into each of the other dishes and she pushes Suzie and I ours. Suzie is looking down at her bowl, but I can see by the expression on her face that for some reason she's disappointed.

"I wanted a large piece. But my problem with pastry is that I'd be as well sticking the raw dough onto my hips, because as soon as I've finished this pie that's where it will end." She starts to chop her ration up into very small pieces.

"You look okay to me Suzie," I had to interject. She looks so sad. I shouldn't have though, should I? I'm just encouraging her and that's naughty. She's blushing, poor thing. I promise I won't do that to her again. I was just getting carried away with the mood of the evening.

"I'm not trying to pry Jenny, but Suzie mentioned

earlier that you've been having nightmares, is that right?" says Paul, wiping his mouth with his napkin. Can you believe it, he's finished his dessert already?

Jenny starts to cough; I mean a serious coughing fit. She's swallowed her pie too quickly and it's gone down her windpipe. Suzie slaps her on the back and Jenny's coughing calms. She sips some of the lemonade that Suzie's poured into a glass for her. Although the tears are streaming down Jenny's face, she seems fine.

I know you thought I would do something angelic like, but sorry, not on this occasion. I'd only intervene if I had thought she was going to die.

"Paul, it's just my imagination playing tricks and Suzie shouldn't have mentioned it." Jenny's voice is husky due to her choking fit.

"Jenny, you're not alone. I've been having some really strange dreams recently. I think we have a mutual problem, and that is that we're both victims of Kurt's bullying," says Paul sensitively. "That's probably what's playing on our minds. I also don't have a terribly happy home life. Although, strangely enough, it has been getting better. Do you have problems at home too?" says Paul confidently.

Way to go, big man. Good on you, he's opening up to his fears. I must be doing something right. Jenny looks so beau…, I mean sad.

"My home life hasn't been so great over the last couple of years. But my mom has come all over caring and we're trying to build bridges. As far as Kurt goes, I probably have to agree. A couple of weeks ago I couldn't have imagined my life without him. But we've been growing apart and I think I'm relieved." There's regret in Jenny's voice.

"You never told me about you and Kurt," interrupts Suzie

"No, I didn't, because you would only mock me." Jenny is provoked by her friend's comment.

"No, I wouldn't, I'm your friend," says Suzie in a raised voice.

"Now, now girls, you're friends, remember that. We four here, are all friends." I don't want to have to make the girls make up again. They can both be as stubborn as mules.

"I'm starting to see things aren't as bad as I first thought they were and especially now I've got three new wonderful friends. I can't tell you three how much I'm enjoying your company and your friendship," says Paul sentimentally.

"I couldn't have said it any better big buddy. It's about realizing that you have friends around you. Friends that can share your problems, share your heavy load. That's what good friends are for," I say that from the heart.

"Oh, Paul and Dan, that's so nice. I think I'm going to cry," says Suzie all doe-eyed.

Let's hope she wants to cry on Paul's shoulder and not mine.

Chapter Twenty

Let him kiss me with the kisses of his mouth.

Song of Songs 1:2

It's Thursday evening, it will soon be the end of another school week. Yippee. You didn't here me say that. Things have been kind of quiet around here the last couple of days. Suspicious? You should be; because I certainly am.

The newly formed four amigos are going out on the town tonight. So watch out Scottsdale, there's trouble coming your way. Ha. Gabriella, minus Kushi, has volunteered to drop us off downtown at around six o'clock. We're heading for the Scottsdale Artwalk tonight.

You're wondering when we all became so highbrow and interested in art? Well we haven't really, it's a school pet project. Our art and music teachers are trying to encourage us to appreciate the finer things in life, like art, music, and ballet.

We're quite happy to go along as it seems that some of the local restaurants give free samples of their wares. If there's free food going down somewhere, my big buddy Paul and I will sniff it out. As we don't turn down freebies. Got to go, I hear a car horn, that'll be my ride now.

§ § §

We've caught the trolley, as we don't feel so energetic. Downtown Scottsdale is really busy tonight. The eateries alongside the canal are heaving with folks. We jump off at Stetson Drive and now we'll head for the Plaza; there's live entertainment there. Us kids haven't had much time to chat since we met up earlier, but I'm sure we'll make up for it now.

"I hope we're not going to leave it too late before we get something to eat," says Paul. Food is never far from his mind.

"Oh Paul." Groan the girls.

"Paul, we're going to become fat because of you," says Suzie.

"Are you not already fat?" teases Paul.

"Huh. I didn't come out tonight to be insulted," says Suzie touchily. She's doing her best to look upset at Paul's remark, but the wry smile on her face assures him that no offense has been taken. Have you noticed that there's a whole lot of flirting going on between my big buddy and Suz? Good for them, they're the perfect couple.

"There will be plenty of time for food later." I endeavor to sweet talk Paul.

"Oh, I suppose so." Paul sounds glum. Everyone laughs and Suzie kisses Paul on the cheek. She links her arm into his and the two of them march ahead towards the sound of the music.

Jenny takes my arm; that strange electrical sensation is shooting through my body. She looks at me and smiles. She kisses me on my cheek. A surge of unchecked feelings rush throughout me.

"It's nice to have some time alone," says Jenny tenderly.

"Is there any reason why we need time to ourselves?" I ask purposely. It's so difficult to pretend that I don't know what she's getting at.

"You can't keep on denying that there's something special between us," says Jenny insistently.

"Jenny, it's called friendship, nothing else."

"Why won't you give in to your feelings?" says Jenny

sulkily.

"Jenny I love you, just as I love Paul and Suzie."

"I've got a battle on my hands with you. But I don't give in that easy." Jenny starts to laugh, her mood has lifted.

"Let's not spoil the evening," I gently say.

"Okay we'll call a truce." She hugs me and I sooo want to kiss her.

"Let's catch up with the other two," I suggest. This whole situation is too heavy.

"Okay, I'll race you. The loser buys dinner, but you need to give me a head start." Jenny darts off at high speed. Of course being the gentleman that I am, I'll make sure she wins. Thank you God.

§ § §

The entertainment this evening has been awesome. We've listened to a Brazilian singer, classical pianist, and now we're being entertained by a brilliant jazz band. The place is absolutely jumping. Wah-whee. We four are boogieing on down, big style. But time is getting on.

"Do we want to catch the next trolley over to Marshall Way and look at the exhibitions?" I ask.

"That's okay by me," says Paul good-humoredly. "How about you girls?" He looks for agreement from the girls.

"Yeahhh!" scream both girls excitedly. Suzie and Jenny link arms, Paul takes Jenny's free arm and I take Suzie's. The four of us start to dance across the concourse. We're causing some people to take notice of us, but they can see our boisterous behavior is all in good fun. I'm sure there will be no stopping us until we reach the awaiting transport. Culture, here we come.

§ § §

We're now in the heart of the Scottsdale Artwalk. To keep Paul happy we've decided to only go to the galleries that are exhibiting food related subject matter. Most of these galleries also have free food sampling stations near or around their entrances. So you can see where I'm coming from. He can fill his belly as well as his eyes and I won't say no to a few samples myself, as I'm starrrving. With any luck we'll all eat so much that I won't have to pay for dinner later. I can't help being a meanie.

§ § §

How do you think I handled the awkward situation with Jenny last night? I was pretty rubbish wasn't I? Nevertheless we all had a fantastic night. Paul has come out of his shell and the girls have really warmed to him. But my job is far from done here and everyday there is a new challenge. I'm still trying to work out what I'm suppose to do about the Red Rider's devotees. Hopefully I'll have some divine inspiration.

Chapter Twenty-One

I do believe; help me overcome my unbelief.

Mark 9:24

It's Saturday today and us kids are all going river rafting on the Verde River. Isais is coming along too. It seems it was something he loved doing with his son. So he's kindly offered to be our taxi for the day. The girls were rather apprehensive, saying they were afraid they would drown. I think that's a rather lame excuse, when we actually all know that they're just scared about getting their hair wet. But finally, with a bit of gentle persuasion, they agreed it would be fun.

We're all strong swimmers, so there should be no problems and hopefully I'll have a helping hand. I can hear Aunt Sylvia calling; breakfast must be ready. Come on and join me, we can catch up. We may not have too much time to chat later.

Stepping out into the hall I can smell fried bacon, which I'm sure is accompanied by pancakes, maple syrup, and a glass of freshly squeezed orange juice. Yum, yum. A growing guy like me needs his vitamin C. Ha.

I'm now in the kitchen and Aunt Sylvia is standing in front of the stove.

"Sit down Dan. Will four pancakes be enough to be going on with for now?" she asks. She's standing with a spatula at the ready in her hand, just in case she needs to rustle up some more.

"Four's fine for now, are you having some?"

"I will have some later. Isais will eat the rest of this batch, if you don't want them." She points to the heaped plate.

"Does Isais know breakfast's ready?" I ask.

"Yes, I rang round." She wipes her hands on her apron.

"While we have a minute, there's something I want to ask you Aunt Sylvia."

"Go ahead Dan, I'm listening." Aunt Sylvia walks over to me, puts her hand on my shoulder, and looks at me attentively.

"Can you tell me if things are going as well as expected?" I ask earnestly.

"The Elders seem fairly pleased, you're progressing well. But you will have to make a decision about the demonlets."

"Yeah, the demonlets. I have to admit that I'm struggling with how to tackle that little problem. I know that they've been possessed by evil, but slaying them is kind of going against the grain.

"I've kept sparring with them, hoping that they're going to change their ways, but that isn't about to happen and if I don't do something sooner, rather than later, they will destroy me. I volunteered for the job, so it looks like I'll have to get on with it."

"Dan, you will be slay...," the door opens and in flounces Isais. It looks like I'll have to finish this conversation another time.

"Good morning and how are you both this fine morning?" He isn't letting on if he heard any of our chat.

"Good morning Isais," Aunt Sylvia and I say together. She walks back to the stove to retrieve the plates she has warming for Isais and I.

"I'm fantastic and I'm really looking forward to our trip today," I say positively.

"Good boy, you will absolutely love it. Unfortunately I have a bit of a sore shoulder today, so I don't think it would be wise for me to join in the activities. But I don't have any problem taking you guys there and taking you on somewhere else when you're all done. I can maybe do a bit of fishing, whilst I'm waiting on you."

"I'm disappointed that you can't take part, and so will the rest of the kids. You won't want to do any more damage. But that will be great if you can join us for some lunch later on and we are grateful for the ride."

"That's settled then," says Isais happily.

Aunt Sylvia places a plate heaped with food in front of us both. It's time for us boys to tuck in. Mmm, Mmm. Bacon.

§ § §

We've just picked up Paul, and we're on our way to Jenny's to pick both the girl's up. Paul is looking rather starry eyed at the thought of seeing Suzie. In fact, I'm probably looking starry eyed at the thought of seeing Jenny. The more I see her, the more I want to throw all caution to the wind. I want to risk everything just to have some quality time with her.

But that would be my heart speaking and not my head. I'm sure that other heavenly beings have also found themselves experiencing human emotions. So I need to deal with it and move on, no matter how difficult it sometimes seems. It's time to remind myself that my experience here is a means to justify an end; the end being the destruction of evil and of course my salvation.

§ § §

We've arrived at Jenny's and Paul has volunteered to go and get the girls. I've never seen him move so fast.

"I thought maybe you had your eye on one of the girls," inquires Isais.

"I've no time for girls Isais."

"Come on boy, a young good looking boy like you

should always leave some time in his life for members of the opposite sex."

"I'm just not ready for dating at present. I just want to get on with my schooling."

"If that's the case, you need to let young Jenny down gently. Because she only has eyes for you."

"I've tried Isais, but she's one stubborn chick."

"As long as you've told her, because that's the right thing to do. You will just need to hope that she finally gets the message and moves her attentions onto someone else. You never know, maybe cupid will give a helping hand and you will have a change of heart. But I'm glad Paul has his sights on young Suzie, because I think she will return his feelings."

I've been so focused on Paul, Jenny, and myself, that I hadn't even noticed that Suzie was growing very fond of my big buddy. He'll be so happy. Less of this chit chat, here they are. I've made sure that there is no room for a small pretty female to slip in the front seat beside me. The small pretty thing being Jenny. I've piled up our waterproof clothing on the spare passenger seat.

"Okay ladies, I'm going to sit in the middle. I want to surround myself with a bevy of beauties. Pile your gear in beside Dan." Paul opens the rear door for the girls.

I'll tell you this kid has really discovered himself. The girls are giggling at his newfound charm as they fling their bags in beside me. I'm staying quiet for a change until the threesome pile into the back seat.

"Buckle up kids, hold on to your hats. Verde River here we come," shouts Isais. You should see the big smug look on his face.

"Altogether now, after three, hip, hip, hooray. One, two three," shouts Paul gleefully.

"Hip, hip, hooray," we all cheer.

§ § §

Weather wise, today is an absolute glorious day. It's an ideal day to go river rafting, as the heat is blistering. Any spray hitting our faces, I'm sure will be welcomed. We've driven around 25 miles and we've arrived at one of the most popular spots of white water outside of Scottsdale. Twelve miles of fast flowing water, just waiting for four kids to have a real cool time.

We're now sitting in the raft; we've all donned our wet suits and life jackets. Our guide and instructor for the day is called Zak. I don't know if Paul and I should be jealous or not, because the girls seem to be very much in awe of him. He is a real handsome dude. He's in his early twenties, so he's practiced his chat up lines for a lot longer than us.

"If you don't mind, we have another party of four joining us. My colleague is just going to hurry them along," says Zak. He's a smiley guy and I would say that he's very comfortable in his own skin. In other words he oozes confidence. The surrounding scenery in the canyon is awesome. Looking around at its natural beauty makes me feel very humble. Suddenly Paul gasps. He's looking more than a little perturbed.

"I don't believe it," he mumbles.

"What?" I'm baffled at the sudden change in attitude.

"Look who's joining us," says Suzie, prodding me in the ribs. She's becoming very animated.

I can't believe my eyes, because you've guessed right, it's the Devil's helpers. Purrrple, purrrple alert. No buzz in my ear though, as my early warning system seems to be very temperamental. Walking behind them is JoJo; she must have brought them along today. I'm guessing that there's trouble brewing. I'm sure I can hear those witches in Shakespeare's play 'Macbeth', cackle.

"I'm sorry Dan, but I don't think I could bear to sit

alongside them." Paul's petrified.

"Paul, don't worry my cuddly amigo, things will be all right. Trust me, believe in me." My words of encouragement aren't assuring him, I can see that. "Group hug, group hug." I'll use some of my angelet power on my friends, these guys need the courage to carry on. We group together and hug and our inflatable is now bobbing about a bit, sorry not a bit, a whole lot. I can feel a surge of power leave my body, hopefully the transference will make my friends more resilient to the powers of evil at work.

"Please stay to the positions you've been allocated, because the raft could capsize. Moving about too much isn't recommended once we're out there. Do not move unless I tell you to," says Zak strictly.

We all shift gently back into our places and my friends are now showing no uneasiness. They've calmed down, amazing what a cuddle can achieve.

"Don't you kids worry none. Everything will be okay." Isais has walked over to us, his words of reassurance are uplifting. Kurt and his three buddies, I use the word buddies loosely, climb in beside us.

"This is a surprise, us all meeting up like this. Especially you Jenny, you've never shown any interest in water sports before," says Kurt derisively.

"Neither did you," answers Jenny abruptly.

"Touché, my little pumpkin. Touché." Kurt laughs causing Jenny's face to flush. Suzie takes hold of her friend's hand in a show of support.

Zak senses there is some tension amongst the group and he says, "Anything personal you kids have going on, I would appreciate that you leave it ashore."

"I can assure you that there will be no trouble today Zak," says Isais convincingly from ashore. I wish I was as confident as he is about the situation. We all sit in silence, like a bunch of naughty school children, except for Kurt who seems to find Isais's optimism rather amusing and is laughing noisily.

Chapter Twenty-Two

The Lord knows how to rescue the godly from trials.

2 Peter 2:9

So far our journey has been rather uneventful, there has been no hocus pocus. I don't know if the calmness of the water has mesmerized the devil's apprentices, or their natural wickedness has been quashed by some magical spell. But all has been quiet on the western front. Then again perhaps the Red Rider is scared his flames will be extinguished if he interferes with the proceedings here. We haven't even had to make small talk with the devotees.

But I can't rest on my laurels; I have to be on my guard at all times. I wish you guys could be here with me, as I could be doing with another set of eyes, preferably in the back of my head. I jest God, about the other set of eyes, as I don't think it would be the makings of a very attractive guy, having two eyes at the back of his bean. If you get my drift. Sorry, think that was a pun, drift, water. Oh you're slow today.

It's quite hard work, this paddling lark, and it's getting even tougher as the flow of the river is getting stronger.

"Right folks, we're approaching mini rapids. You need to follow my instructions carefully. Sit tight and enjoy," shouts Zak. We can hardly hear him over the noise of the fast moving water. The raft is now really bobbing about and the looks of concentration on Jenny and Suzie's faces are intense. Paul is looking very uncomfortable, I don't know if it's the motley crew that he's afraid of, or the rapids ahead. We hit the mini rapids with a bump.

"Sweep your strokes, sweep your strokes. Come

on; pull your blade through the water. Sit down low," instructs Zak.

We make our way through the torrent of water and Suzie stifles a scream. Our raft seems to struggle to keep upright as we dip violently up and down. Our speed is escalating and the rubber bottom of our raft bangs against the water surface. Faster, faster we go; it's like riding the big dipper. *Slap, slap,* that's the sound of our inflatable bouncing, bouncing. I'm feeling kind of sick; shouldn't have had those extra pancakes, or mmm, the bacon, or the sticky maple syrup.

The water hits our faces. Oh, heck, they've picked a hell of a time to change into, aaagh, purrrple mo… I can't even say the word as I just left my stomach at the last bump. *Whoosh,* the force of the water batters our raft off the rocks. It's difficult to remain seated; Suzie is sent hurtling to the opposite side of the raft and her paddle drops into the water. Zak catches hold of her life jacket and pulls her back into her position.

Kurt has now changed into his alter ego and his accomplices have nearly completed their transformation. I don't know how I'm going to pull this one off. Any ideas? Sorry, no time to think, or confer. I can't even tweet a friend. Kurt and friends throw their paddles aside and the girls are squealing with terror.

Paul seems to have frozen to the spot and Zak looks as though he's seen a ghost. I don't really know if they're seeing the same situation as I am, but by the looks on their faces, they know there is something amiss.

My spirit has left my body and I'm trying to catch hold of Kurt, but he's a sneaky devil. His pincer's snap, snap at me all the time, but I dodge him easily. Robbie Dillon is grabbing hold of Paul and he's trying to push him over the side. They're grappling, but Paul will never compete with the strength of the new Robbie. I need to assist him, but I'm finding it difficult to contain Kurt.

I don't know how this raft is still afloat, because only the girls and my human form are still seated. They're hanging on like grim death and my body is bouncing about all over the place. Water is filling the raft; if we don't capsize we'll probably sink. I swipe at Kurt, I manage to touch him and temporarily render him powerless.

Robbie and the two other disciples are trying to heave Paul over the side. Zak is trying to help Paul, but he's no match for them. He's flung clear to the opposite side and narrowly avoids going overboard. Our boat spins; round and round we go.

I'm struggling to reach Paul, but I'm stretching my particle arms out and I've succeeded in circling Robbie and friends. But they're strong and I'm finding it difficult to hold onto them. Paul's body balances on the edge of the raft, it's only his grasp of Robbie that now stops him from plunging into the water.

Remarkably I've halted Robbie and his aides, I'm using all my strength to pull them back, away from the side of the raft. Robbie has let go of Paul and Paul slides back onto the floor of the raft. But as we move uncontrollably through the white bubbling water, I lose my grip on Robbie and he bounces back to life. His pincers swipe at me and his tail bends forward on attack.

Suddenly, as I go on the defense, I'm pulled from behind. Kurt has come to the aid of Robbie. I have to free myself from him before we all fade away into oblivion. I'm not worried about my fate; after all I'm already dead. I just want to save my friends. Kurt is weak; I force him back without much difficulty. Hopefully he will remain useless for the time being.

My altercation with Kurt means that Paul has been left in the lap of God. Once again, he's struggling with Robbie. My big buddy is gripping onto the rope that's attached to the side of the raft in an effort to save himself. But I can see the stringy fibers of the rope are burning into the palms of his hands and he may not be able to hold on for much longer. I'm battling with Robbie now, but Paul has lost his grip and he plummets into the foaming liquid below. I can see his arms disappear below the surface and he's been swallowed into the depths.

Robbie is exhausted and has collapsed onto the floor of our boat, which means I can focus on saving Paul. Unexpectedly, the waters have calmed and the raft is bobbing gently, thankfully we're hardly moving.

"Paul, Paul," I shout his name. Okay you know that's his name, I'm just being a klutz. There's no sign of him, the girl's are still screaming. They've never stopped. I'm not confident that I can walk on water, I think that skill is reserved for the Lamb of God. Therefore I need to go back to the drawing board, if I'm going to save my friend.

Out of nowhere, an enormous bald eagle has swooped down; it's submerging its great legs deep down into the water, as though fishing for salmon. It's pulling up slowly, baldy guy has caught something. He's flapping his wings like mad to raise himself, and his catch, clear of the water. Whew, his catch is Paul and a couple of catfish. His claws are wrapped around my big buddies shoulders, holding him safe and securely. The tail of the fish is hitting Paul in the face; I would laugh if the circumstances weren't so dangerous.

The eagle continues to flap his massive wings, squawking as it hovers above us. Its shadow covers our boat, shading us from the burning sun. It gently drops an unconscious Paul into our rubber craft and it flies off with its fish catch. I touch Paul's arm; he coughs and splutters, water fountains out of his mouth. Thank God, he's alive.

§ § §

As we paddle gently back to where our adventure started, I see Isais sitting on the riverbank, he's in the process of unhooking a large flathead catfish from his fishing line. The fish isn't dissimilar to the one that the bald eagle caught along with Paul.

Talking of eagles, if that big guy hadn't come along, I don't know what would have happened. He was so huuuge that he wouldn't have been out of place in a 3D movie about dinosaurs.

Zak jumps out of our boat into the shallow water. His partner ashore joins him and the two men guide our raft onto the stony shore.

"Good to see you kids back safely. Did you have a good time?" says Isais with a big grin on his face. Everyone's clambering out of the boat, I'm feeling kind of unsteady on my feet.

"We had an awesome time. No real mishaps, other than Suzie losing her paddle, and Paul nearly taking a swim. But otherwise we're all safe and sound. How about you?" I smile wryly.

"I've been enjoying fishing in this well stocked part of the river. We've got plenty of catfish for tea, although the last one I caught was a bit tricky. As you can see my trousers are rather wet, he did a bit of splashing about, before I netted him." He turns his attention to Kurt and friends and he says, "Bad news kids, JoJo had an emergency and she had to leave. I would offer you a lift home, but unfortunately I've no more room in my truck."

"Yes, that's unfortunate. Did she say how she expected us to get home?" asks Kurt cynically. If you could see the look on purple boy's face. He's looking just slightly disgruntled.

"No boy, but I'm sure if you call one of your parents they'll come and get you."

"Thanks for not causing any problems today Kurt. For once you acted like an adult," says Jenny. But he ignores her praise.

I start to cough, something seems to be sticking in my throat; it's probably Jenny's naive words. Thank goodness she and the others in my group, including Zak, don't seem to have any recollection of our narrow escape from death. Well, their narrow escape from death.

Kurt and clan look rather puzzled at the mysterious disappearance of their mentor. We'll just have to wait and see how the mystery unfolds. Hopefully she's flown off on her broomstick somewhere and she's never coming back. But I think that's just wishful thinking on my behalf. What do you think? Email me.

Chapter Twenty-Three

"Whoever comes to me I will never drive away."

John 6:37

The rest of the gang are unusually quiet, but I'll just put that down to their supply of adrenalin having dried up; for today anyway. I know I'm exhausted, so they must be too. Paul had a miraculous escape from death today; I lost control of the situation and failed to keep my friends safe.

I believe, because of my failings, there was divine intervention and that's the only reason why they're still here with me tonight. Basically it wasn't their time to go. I apologize for coming over all morose, in fact my mood is morbid, mixed with a huge dollop of frustration, not cream, as is my normal preference.

When I saw that bald eagle, I was sure he was on the devil's side. I thought he was going to eat my big buddy. But thankfully he didn't, although it still doesn't answer my question as to where the big baldy guy came from, or who actually sent him. The plot thickens. I need to have a real serious talk with Aunt Sylvia tonight.

"So are you kids up for catfish done Navajo style?" Isais breaks the silence.

"Thanks for the offer, but could I make it another night?" Suzie is the first to respond.

"Sure Suzie, of course you can, anytime you want."

"I'm absolutely beat and I'd like to call it a day," says Paul.

"I'm up for it, if Dan is," says Jenny, but rather lethargically.

"It's all down to you boy, how about it?" Isais sounds rather disappointed.

I truly appreciate his offer, but if it's only Jenny and I going along. Well, enough said.

"Sorry I don't want to be a party pooper, but I'd rather make it another night when we can all enjoy the good food, without falling asleep." I was in two minds, but my sensible mind made the decision.

"Okay it will probably be for the best. I'm pretty bushed anyway," agrees Jenny.

"That's a date kids; I'll just take you home," says Isais ungrudgingly.

"You could drop Paul and I off at Jenny's place and we can make our way home from there. If that's fine with you Isais?" says Suzie.

"If you're sure. Whatever you kids wish, is my command. I'll stick the biggest catfish in the freezer and we can have it another time. As long as you're not making excuses because you're scared of my cooking," says Isais, chuckling heartily.

§ § §

Isais has dropped the others off and we're making our way back to the house.

"You're pretty subdued tonight Dan, is there anything bothering you?" asks Isais with a note of fatherly concern in his voice.

"Everything is fine Isais," I fib.

"Come on, you can tell me. I was young once you know."

"Honestly, Isais, everything is real cool."

"Even that big bald headed eagle you saw today? Was he real cool too?"

My mind is in a whirl, how the heck can he know

about the eagle? I don't know what to say to him. I'm just staring out of the window, because I'm gob smacked. Totally and utterly gob smacked.

"Has the cat got your tongue boy?"

"No. I just don't understand how you know about the eagle. Do you want to explain?"

"I'll do my best, but it's pretty complicated. It's as complicated as you being a trainee angel."

I'm absolutely dumbfounded, as well as gob smacked, at what he's just said. Did you have any idea that he knew my secret? He must be an angel, otherwise how would he know that? He could be the Devil for all I know. That's it, my covers blown and I'm going to hell. I've been fraternizing with the enemy.

"I can see that you are pretty shocked Dan." That was rather an understatement from Isais.

"I'd like you to explain to me how you know about the eagle, please."

"Fair enough boy, I realize that what I've said has come as a shock to you. So I better start explaining. As you know I'm a Navajo. In our folklore skin-walkers are very much talked about. In fact, they're common in one form or another in most Native American legends, just as werewolves are prominent in English lore.

The fact is I'm a yee naaldlooshii, being the Navajo word for skin-walker. Please don't say that there is no such thing, because I would have to say that some say there is no such thing as angels. But I won't, because I know there are."

"I don't really know anything about skin-walkers, other than they're witches of sorts."

"Okay I won't force you to admit you're not human. We'll leave that disputed point for now. A skin-walker is also known by some as a shape shifter, because we can change our shape into something else. The something else, normally being the form of an animal. What I'm saying is that, the eagle you saw today was me."

"This disclosure has come to me as a grandiose shock, Isais."

"I'm sure it has boy. I knew there was every chance you would need some help when I saw JoJo and her boys arrive. That's when I decided to follow you, overhead. You weren't doing too badly until Paul fell in the river.

"I knew you weren't going to be able to save him in time, that's when I had to step in. I hope I haven't spoiled things for you, by doing so. But I did it for all the right reasons."

"I guessed that you would just do spells and stuff. I didn't think you would do things to benefit others."

"I found God many years ago. I was desperate and he didn't turn me away, he was there when I needed him. At that point I stopped practicing the witchery way.

"I vowed I would never use my black magic powers again. But, young Dan, you and your friends came into my life and I couldn't sit back and allow innocents to be destroyed. The first time I met JoJo I knew that the Devil was at work, after all I had practiced her craft for many years myself."

"Is Aunt Sylvia aware of your identity?"

"I don't know. I'm sure she must be, because I'm aware she has her own powers. But I have a feeling that although she accepts me, because of my past, she's treading cautiously."

"I appreciate what you did for my friends today, but how do I know you are not lulling me into a false sense of security and you're actually in cahoots with Satan? I mean, it's not as though I can call God and ask him for a reference."

"But when you looked me up on your little gadget, did you discover anything bad about me?"

"No, but I didn't find anything out about JoJo either. By the way, do you have any inkling why she left?"

"JoJo and I had a slight altercation, serpents are fair game for bald eagles. She ran scared, left her protégés to fend for themselves. She'll be back, if she's not stopped.

"But for now, it's not her I want to discuss boy; I want to talk about our relationship. Relationships are built on trust and I know I can't make you trust me Dan, but I hope and pray, that you can eventually. If there is anything I can do to prove my integrity, please ask."

"I think I'll sleep on it for tonight."

"Okay, I won't mention our chat again unless you want to. We're home, I won't come in. I'll pray that you can accept me for who I am, as God has. I hope that you will believe I have no hidden agenda."

"Goodnight, Isais."

"Goodnight, boy. God bless." Isais watches me as I jump out of the truck, leaving him sitting alone in the cab. I can tell you I'm absolutely blown away after the events of today. Believe it or not, my conversation with Isais has proven even more mind blowing than fighting demons. I'm definitely going to have to sleep on it. Optimistically without nightmares.

Chapter Twenty-Four

"I am young in years, and you are old; that is why I was fearful, not daring to tell you what I know."

Job 32:6

"That old black magic's got me in its spell, do.do. do. That..." Sorry about my terrible singing. Arlen and Mercer would cringe if they heard my rendition. I'm certainly not singing like an angel today, that's for sure.

Have you ever woken up with a song in your head, that you can't shake off? Yup, much to my disappointment and I'm sure God's, I can't shake those lyrics. Even if I start to sing a Psalm, those words just keep on interrupting my holy thoughts.

The thing is, I'm still pretty shaken at the goings on at the Verde River. So much so, that I hid away all day yesterday. I told Aunt Sylvia that I just wanted to get my head down and think certain things through. I even avoided boring you with my drivel.

I didn't disclose to my guardian the actual details of my preoccupation, but she didn't pry and seemed cool with the whole situation. Probably because she understands the trials and tribulations of being an angel, or would be angel.

I was under no real pressure to meet up with any of the other kids either, as we've seen quite a bit of each other over the last couple of days. Not that we're bored of each other, as if. Oh no, the reason being that there's the small thing of homework assignments that need to be completed. On Sundays I usually knuckle down and cram, cram, cram. After church of course.

We only exchanged brief text messages, although

Suzie was exempt from that statement. You know her as well as I do now, she just can't stop communicating. So, if she's told not to call, she'll text and when our Suzie texts, she writes a thesis. She also expects a reply straight away.

But the whole texting thing was cool with me yesterday, as it meant that no little white lies were forthcoming from my angelic mouth. Thank goodness for small blessings.

Listen, can we talk later? I know it sounds as though I'm fobbing you off with excuses, but I really do have a lot going on inside my head and my pea-sized brain is in danger of overloading, or imploding.

If I share every minute, intricate detail that's whirling around, you'll close this book, never to flick open a page again. A page of my story anyway. So let's talk later, at school.

§ § §

Isais's Story

Isais is wearing buck skin trousers. On his broad shoulders drapes a black and white sheepskin. His feathered headdress is made of white feathers with black tips. His deeply tanned face is painted white with black lines on each cheek. He wails his ceremonial song,

"Ahehee', ahehee', ahehee'."

Opening a small leather pouch, he removes some small animal teeth. Placing them in a stone mortar and pestle, he begins to pound them.

"Mmm, mmm, mmm," he hums tunelessly as he does so.

He pounds, pounds, and pounds. Beating the teeth until they become a fine powder. Pulling out the cork of a miniature opaque glass bottle he retrieved from another leather pouch, he trickles its syrupy contents into the mortar. He stirs the mixture with his index finger until it resembles a thick paste.

He draws his pasty finger along the edge of the bowl to remove the residual concoction that's sticking to it. Isais then places the vessel on to a small hand-woven rug on the floor beside a small bone spoon. Kneeling down beside them, he raises his arms in the air and he starts to sing incoherently, "Aaagh, aaagh, aaagh, awoo', cha, awoo, cha, bijeeh, cha, bijeeh."

Lifting the spoon he scoops up some of the mixture from the mortar and places it into his mouth. He doesn't chew, he swallows it straight down. He picks up some more and eats it. The mortar is now nearly empty. He scrapes his spoon around the sides of the bowl, but before taking the last mouthful he recites some magic words,

"Abid, atsoo', cha, ahehee'."

§ § §

Do you remember when Aunt Sylvia advised me never to trust anyone? She explained that the Red Rider comes in all shapes and sizes. That's my particular quandary at present. Although Isais has never presented himself to me as a foot soldier, or a field commander of the Devil's army, I can't put my trust in him. Can I?

He comes across as a real nice dude, but after all, beauty is only skin deep and he could be a wolf in sheep's clothing. If you dig my train of thought.

I've decided I'm not going to discuss Isais with Aunt Sylvia because I think this is one enigma that I need to fathom out for myself. It could be part of the entrance exam to heaven and I don't want the score of nil, for naivety, or for being a jerk first class.

I can't overlook Isais's admission of having practiced witchcraft in the past and the info that was downloaded to us makes me think he still does. There's also the incident of him mutating into a humongous bald eagle. That occurrence was not for the faint hearted, I can tell you. The teachings of my Holy Book tell me that godliness and witchcraft don't mix, and for now, I have to run with that.

§ § §

Thanks for being so understanding earlier today, you're a real good friend. Since you're still with me, you didn't throw the book to the floor or slide it back onto the bookshelf to gather dust. You couldn't have deleted me from your eReader either. You stayed, and I want you to know that you're very much appreciated. Enough of my crawling, let's get going.

§ § §

We're all assembled in drama class; did you know in this guy Hemingway's book there's an awful lot of grown-up stuff going down? But clever Miss Summerville has managed to do a fantastic adaptation and she's spared our blushes. Otherwise, I'm not so sure it would be appropriate for a high school stage play. The kids would love it, but the parents would be making lots of "Tut, Tut," sounds.

I know the book is a great American classic and I definitely don't dispute that. But it has caused some controversy in the past. OMG, listen to me, I'm sounding like a grumpy old man. OMG, maybe I was an old grump. Okay, okay, I'll shut up. Do you think I was an old grump? Ha-ha, got you.

There's an awful lot of noise in the classroom. On Monday's we all like to exchange our weekend experiences and today is no different. But as you know there are certain events of my weekend that aren't up for discussion.

"Quiet, settle down," shouts Miss Summerville. The room doesn't fall into complete silence, the noise of muted talk, shuffling of feet and papers, still circulates around. "I said quiet," shouts Miss Summerville again. The room falls silent. "Dan, will you please give the rest of the class a quick résumé of the scene we're about to start." She's now easily heard.

I'm really glad I read through this last night, otherwise I would look like a proper nitwit. "Right, Dan, on you go," encourages Miss Summerville.

I stand up and clear my throat. The usual suspects giggle around the room.

"Henry has deserted the Italian army. After borrowing civilian clothes from his friend Sim, he travels from Milan to Stressa by train. He's hoping to meet up with Catherine, who is now heavily pregnant." On my last word I hear more snickering from the girls.

"Carry on Dan, ignore your childish classmates." Miss Summerville looks around the room in disapproval.

I take a sharp intake of breath. "Um, she's in Stressa with her close friend, Helen Ferguson. Henry asks around as to her whereabouts and he finally goes to a hotel where he finds Catherine and Helen eating supper. Catherine is delighted to see him, but Scottish born, Helen is angry with both of them and she becomes very emotional.

"She's upset because they're both so blasé about their affair and the impending birth out of wedlock. Eh, I think that's the general gist of the next act."

"Thank you, Dan, for that. That was spot on. Right, let's get started."

Chapter Twenty-Five

Those who practice magic arts, the idolaters and all liars-their place will be in the fiery lake of burning sulfur.

Revelation 21:8

Demon's Story

It's 7 am, and JoJo transmutes from her serpent appearance into that of her human form. She dresses quickly into her canteen assistant's uniform and makes her way into the kitchen at the back of her house. The sun is rising, causing the cacti in her backyard to imitate shadowy figures, which move desultorily across the ground.

A transient shadow makes her stop what she's doing. She lifts up the net curtain, to take a second look out of the window. She can't see anything incongruous and she drops the window covering back into place.

She goes into the utility room to get her white leather clogs from the shoe rack. An indistinguishable figure flashes across the opaque glass of the door that leads to the yard. JoJo turns the key in the lock clockwise and then opens the door with some caution. There are no obvious visible signs of her having uninvited company. But nevertheless, she steps out onto the paved path that circles the house and calls out,

"Hello, is there someone there?"

Only the crickets chirp a reply. She laughs raucously and turns to go back inside. Bang, the clatter of a garbage can comes from the side of the house. She moves towards the location of the noise gingerly.

"Grrr, grrr, grrr." A male black bear appears from around the corner, causing JoJo to jump back in surprise. The bear stands upright on its long hind legs and begins to walk towards

JoJo. Its broad skull and large jaws seem disproportionate to its three and a half foot stature. The curved claws of its leathery soled forepaws gouge at the air, forcing JoJo to backtrack her steps speedily.

She goes back into the utility room, but she has no time to close the door as the bear is close behind. The black omnivore swipes at her, but misses his target. JoJo commences her mutation, but doing so lessens her ability to stay out of the bears reach. He catches hold of her shoulder, she squeals as the razor-sharp claws dig deep into her flesh.

She frees herself from his clutches, she has only partially changed into her demon state. The bear aims a blow at JoJo's twisting serpent like head. His sharp nails meet with their objective once again. This time tearing at the scaly skin on top of her head.

The demon is using up all her energy to fight for her existence, meaning that her full metamorphosis is being delayed. The black bear has the upper hand and JoJo's powers are all but depleted. She has nowhere to go and nowhere to hide. She can only hope that her master can forgive her for her weakness.

§ § §

Another day another dollar, as the saying goes. Heck knows why I just said that, because it has no relevance whatsoever to my school day. Do all these expressions pop into my head because of my past life, or because I'm a Muppet? Smarty pants, I didn't really want you to reply. Sometimes you're very forward and unquestionably bold.

I've had a long boooring morning in Art class. You just have to see my masterpiece. It's not to everyone's taste, especially the art teacher's. But hey, I think it's got merit. I'm another Pablo Picasso in the making. Well maybe I exaggerate a little.

Sorry, I forgot to tell you where I am; I'm in the dining

hall, waiting on the rest of the crowd. Well not exactly a crowd; there's four of us in total. I'm using what I think they call a generalization. I've no time for this small talk; here comes Paul and Jenny and they're looking very upbeat. Another thing that slipped my mind; demon JoJo has been posted missing today. Surprised? You shouldn't be if you read the download, or are you skipping pages?

I can't say for certain who destroyed her, but I can hazard a guess and if you can't, well I'm not going to be the one that spills the beans. I'm good at keeping secrets; you should know that by now. Okay, maybe I'll tell you later. I know if I don't, you'll harp on it all day and night. On, on, on, on… Here they are.

"Hi, guys. You two are looking very happy today."

As usual Paul's tray is piled high with goodies and Jenny's looks as though food rationing has come into play. Paul thumps his tray down opposite me and Jenny slides hers beside mine.

"Jenny was just laughing at my poor singing voice. We've been in music class all morning. I've told her we all have different tastes in music and she doesn't appreciate my baritone vocals." Paul wrestles into his seat.

"Baritone vocals my foot, you're tone deaf," says Jenny impudently.

"I agree I may be slightly musically challenged, but I'm not that bad. My gran says I'm good," says Paul protectively.

"Don't you think your gran may be slightly biased?" I ask.

"No I don't think so. She's normally very honest with her opinions," says Paul genuinely.

Jenny and I burst into laughter. Paul's looking rather annoyed with us; he decides not to comment and he starts to tuck into his meat loaf. Jenny and I are just sitting watching him. He's stopped chomping and he's looking up from his plate. I think the big grin on his face shows that all is forgiven. A blob of tomato sauce sits in the middle of his chin. I won't tell him just now, I'll wait a while. That's what I love about my friends; we have so much fun together.

"Jen, where's Suzie?" It's just clicked with me that Suzie hasn't joined us as yet. She should have been in class with these guys.

"She texted me this morning saying she wasn't feeling too good. Thinks she's coming down with the flu," answers Jenny.

"That's not so good. Hope she hasn't given us any of her germs," I say.

"I agree, I hate when I have the cold, or flu," says Paul. Just as he's about to put another piece of loaf into his mouth, something has dawned on him. "Jenny, that means you'll have to play Catherine today."

OMG, amour alert. The scene we're rehearsing is real passionate. Jenny and I are going to have to get up real close. My feelings towards Jenny are still running high and the last thing I want to do is to recite romantic dialogue to her. Hopefully I'll come down with the flu in the next ten minutes. If you have the bug, breathe on me, breathe on me, sneeze, sneeze. No good, I still feel okay.

I've had a brain wave. I won't tell Paul about the sauce on his face until we're in class; then he'll be so mad with me, that he'll punch me on the nose. Meaning that, I most certainly will spend the rest of the day in the nurse's office. Hey presto, no love scene.

Lame idea I know, but I don't hear you coming up with any better ones.

Chapter Twenty-Six

O God…cleanse me from my sin.

Psalm 51:1, 2

Isais's Story

Isais is sitting cross legged on his bedroom floor, rocking back and forth, back and forth, whilst moaning a Navajo dirge. His eyes are glazed over, as though he's in a trance. He begins to stroke a bear skin, which is lying across his knees and then he gently starts to separate the clumps of fur with his fingers; his actions don't seem to have any real purpose.

The radio is playing in the background, but he hasn't been listening. The volume increases all of a sudden , causing Isais to stop and take notice. A jingle plays and the announcer on the local station informs his listeners that he has an important announcement to make.

"The Police department have today posted a warning to the residents in the Green Gables neighborhood of Scottsdale, following the death of local woman JoJo Apollyon-Bruta. Miss Apollyon-Bruta is believed to have been killed by a black bear, which was seen in the vicinity, around daybreak. The fatal injuries she sustained are said to coincide with that of an attack by a member of the American black bear family. Therefore Police believe they can rule out homicide.

"Neighbors say although she was fairly new to the neighborhood, she was a popular resident. Especially with the kids at Wingate High, where she was a senior catering manager. Miss Apollyon-Bruta is believed to live alone and not known to have any family or relatives.

"Police ask that the residents of Green Gables stay vigilant until the bear is caught and destroyed. So folks keep those

windows and doors locked."

The news flash ends and a pop song begins to stream out of the radio. Isais starts to sing his dirge again. Only this time his voice seems to exude a more celebratory tone.

§ § §

Holy cow, this dude Hemingway and I have a lot in common. He was only eighteen months older than I am at present when he was wounded in Italy. Luckily for him it wasn't fatal and he didn't become a spiritual being at an early age. I certainly couldn't imagine going off to war. God bless those who do though. Now, pay attention to what I'm trying to tell you and don't go yawning on me again.

This smart dude was part of a group of Writers and Artists known as the Lost Generation based in Paris, France. Although as far as I know I've never been to France, I'm part of a Lost Generation aren't I? Okay, okay; I'm perfectly aware that on occasions my head's filled with minced beef. So let's move on.

A kissing scene is imminent, therefore I've been gargling with peppermint mouthwash. Why? Well even angelets suffer from nap mouth when they wake up in the morning and I've not been able to shake mine so far today. Must pay a visit to a dentist soon.

§ § §

The news is out; JoJo won't be serving meat loaf and tomato sauce ever again in Wingate High. The place is buzzing with the news. She was a very popular lady with the kids. I use the term lady very loosely, because as we both know she was no true lady. I always found her a bit slimy myself.

I'm slightly relieved by her demise. Question for you; were you shocked when you found out that Isais was the one who eradicated her? Good; glad you're keeping up with events. The thing I can't get my head round, is why he's doing this? If you have the answer let me know ASAP. To think that the work of the Red Rider is now finished in Wingate would be a tad foolish. There's likely to be new and more challenging challenges ahead. Watch this space.

Whoa, I need to fill you in as to where I'm at present. It's full blown amour alert, it's drama class time. Gooorgeous Jenny is over the other side of the room going over her lines. I'm desperately trying not to drool as I look over at her. Oh heck, I think I'm going to get in deep dodo from my superiors. Angelets aren't allowed to drool, that's too human. Here we go kids, wish me luck.

"Center stage, Dan and Jenny. Jenny's standing in for Suzie today. Hush, hush. Dan and Jenny, places please. Come on hush now, please," demands Miss Summerville. You could hear a pin drop, the room is so quiet. Jenny and I are sitting either side of a small metal bistro type table, which has been covered in a piece of checked gingham for authenticity. We're supposed to be sitting in a small cafe in Switzerland. So use your imagination. I swallow hard because I know I'm going to get that strange sensation deep down in my stomach when I look into Jen's big sensual eyes.

Wow. I've done it; I've looked into her gooorgeous eyes and it was even worse than I thought it was going to be. My tummy feels as though I'm riding on a roller coaster, simultaneously doing a bungee jump from the Grand Canyon Skywalk. Awesome.

"Darling, are you happy?" Jenny smiles at me. Her cute mouth crinkles at the edges and she places her hand on top of my forearm.

"Yes very, darling," I say sincerely.

"We can have a hearty feast before we are arrested." She looks deep into my eyes.

"Don't worry darling, we are American and British citizens. Once we hand over our papers, everything will be okay." I lift her hand and raise it to my mouth, and I kiss the tip of her fingers gently. Boom shakalaka, I've bungee jumped straight down the Grand Canyon. "I love you J… Catherine."

"I love you too, darling."

I lean across the small tabletop and I lift her chin gently, so that I can look into her beautiful face. I brush away a stray strand of her blonde hair from her cheek. My whole body trembles.

Her eyes are locked into mine. Closer, closer I move. I can smell her sweet perfume. Sorry, can't give you the brand, as we angelets have our limitations. Her cheeks are glowing. Her lips are pink and moist. I can feel her breath. Closer, closer, it's time for the move kids. Done, done, I've kissed her.

"Dan and Jenny, that was great I felt the emotion, the love. But Dan, you're suppose to kiss her on the mouth not the nose. Next time okay," says Miss Summerville.

Come on, you didn't think I was going to really kiss her, did you? Naughty, naughty.

§ § §

I'm over in Apache Park, on North 85th Place. I'm playing soccer for the Wingate Rams today. Paul and Jenny are standing on the sidelines, they'll be lending the team some well needed support. Suzie can't be here, because she's still feeling rather under the weather, so we're being deprived of her wonderful company today. I must pay her a visit later.

Speaking of depraved rather than deprived, the opposition team has just arrived. The other kids in my team have been speaking non-stop about our opponent's new star player. Isais hasn't been able to find anything out about the kid, but I now realize why. The star player in question is Kurt. Well, at least he won't have JoJo along for support.

I don't know how Paul and Jenny are going to react when they catch sight of him. He's looking rather purple so I can say for certain that this game of soccer isn't going to be straight forward, by no manner of means.

§ § §

A pre-selected player from each of our teams are standing on the center circle of the soccer pitch and they shake hands. The referee throws a coin in the air and asks the players to call heads or tails. The opposition team wins the call and their player chooses to kick the match off. He kicks the ball from the center spot to one of his players to start the game. Wow they're on the attack. Away we go.

Even though there is only a small group of spectators, the atmosphere is pretty electrifying, as they're all chanting support for their team. Hey this team is good; they're passing the ball from player to player and making their way up towards the goalposts without faltering. So far, Kurt is just Kurt, he's not transformed completely into his purple form.

The defense players on my team are easily out maneuvered in their attempts to block the progress of the ball. I'm hanging about the center line hoping that one of my team mates will intercept the ball and I can show off my skills. Yahoo, one of my team mates has managed to get the ball and he's kicked it, yep, straight to me.

As I run with the ball down the middle of the pitch, I'm feeling pretty confident that I can put this in the back of the net. Nearer, nearer, I'm nearing the 18 yard box, I'm within shooting distance and I pull back my leg. But what's happened? I can't move my leg. I look down and a purple pincer has a real tight grip of my ankle.

Looking quickly around, I've realized I'm totally

outnumbered by demonlets. The whole of the opposing team has changed into various strange looking creatures and purple seems to be the favored shade of skin tone. I don't know what to do, other than carry on playing the game. I'm at a loss. I don't know if leaving my human form would be advantageous. Too many bad guys for me to contend with.

I kick the ball towards the goalmouth, but a huge guy with two heads blocks it and the ball bounces straight back to me. Holy cow; I try to move with the ball and a pincer swipes past my head. *Whoosh,* that was another arm like thing just missing me. Guys, I don't know if I'm going to get out of this game alive. Get praying kids. No matter who your god is, pray.

Wow, your prayer must have been heard. A huge spotted hyena has appeared from nowhere. His head is absolutely e-nor-mous. Man you should see his teeth. Actually, you'd better not.

Spotty dog has just lifted the two headed guy in his mouth. Oooh, those strong jaws are going to snap him in two. Oh well, he'll have a head for each half of the pitch. That's if he snaps him down the middle, that is. He's shaking him like he's a rag doll.

Whoosh, ha, I saw that coming Kurty. Here he comes again, this time Robbie has joined forces with him. But Robbie has a surprise in store. Yep, Spotty dog has just thrown Robbie in the air. Kurt's tail is coming towards me and the spike on the end of it looks deadly. He's hissing, can you hear him?

Whoosh, I've managed to dodge Kurt again. I've ran behind him, and he's turning clumsily around. *Swipe,* whoa, he's managed to stab me with that tail. I can feel my strength depleting. Oh heck, I feel kind of woozy; I made a mistake not transforming. I drop to the ground like a brick and Kurt's standing over me. His arcing tail is heading for me again. Aaagh.

Thank God, Spotty has come to my rescue. His jaws are clamped around Kurt's body. He's shaking him, shaking him, shaking, shaking. I'm struggling to keep my eyes open. Zzz, zzz.

Chapter Twenty-Seven

Be strong and courageous. …for the Lord your God will be with you wherever you go.

Joshua 1:9

Had you worried, didn't I? Thankfully, Spotty saved me. I hope you realized my new hyena friend was Isais. Duh, how could you not?

Moving on; when I came to, Isais was no longer Spotty and he was sponging my forehead with cold water. Paul was trying to help me by wafting smelling salts underneath my nose. Yuck. No real injuries, other than my pride. Kurty boy was taken to the hospital with a suspected broken collar bone, but the rest of his team just had a few scrapes and bruises.

Paul, Jenny, and the other spectator's take on the incident was slightly different from the reality. They were under the impression that Kurt, I, and some of the other players got into some sort of skirmish. With me being the guy who was getting a good beating. It seems that Isais bravely stepped in and pulled my attackers off me. So keep the real version of events to yourself. Aunt Sylvia said that she's worried for my safety and I need to stay alert. I'm baffled as to why she still hasn't mentioned that Isais's a skin-walker. I'm also amazed at his versatility, imagine being able to transmute into all different types of animals; eagles, bears that kill, and hyenas. What next?

Jenny was very quiet about everything and I'm hoping that wasn't a sign that she was upset about Kurt's injuries. I say that, because she didn't exactly look too worried about my state of health and she hasn't shown any interest in Suzie's wellbeing.

I called Suzie's place earlier, and her mom said that Suz is pretty poorly, so that's where I'm going right now. I'm going slightly earlier than planned, because I'm expecting Paul to join me at some point and I really want to try and have some private time with her.

§ § §

"So how are you, Suzie?" I can tell you, she isn't looking too hot. She's lying flat out in bed and her bedroom is in semi darkness.

"Oh, Dan, how nice of you to pop round," she says as she struggles to sit up in bed. I help her sit up by propping a pillow behind her head and then I sit down on the bed beside her. She continues, "Dan, I've never felt so bad in my life. The doctor said that he thinks I must have some kind of viral infection."

"Has he done any tests?"

"He did some blood tests, but nothing showed up there. He's just told me to take some bed rest for a couple of days."

"Why are the blinds pulled Suzie?"

"The light was hurting my eyes. I don't have a rash, so he ruled out meningitis. I just don't have any energy and I seem to be getting weaker. The doc said I was to just lie with my eyes closed. But the thing is, I don't really want to, because when I do, I see all sorts of strange creatures.

"The doc says I'm having some sort of hallucinations. At first he thought I had a temperature, but my temp is normal." Suzie's voice is beginning to wane and she starts to cry.

"Come on, Suz. What's happened to my beautiful girl? The girl that hangs around me like a bad smell." I take hold of her hand.

"Oh, that's nice. I've had a few unflattering things said about me in my time. But to call me a 'bad smell'."

She laughs weakly.

I stroke away her tears, gently with my thumb. "Suzie, it's an endearing term. Please believe me." I kiss her on top of the head and she sighs.

"I love you, Dan." She closes her eyes and she settles further down into the feathery pillow.

"I love you too, Suz." I kiss each of her eye-lids gently; I can taste the salt of her tears. She sighs again. Slipping my shoes off, I sidle close beside her on the bed. Whoa, whoa, stop thinking what you're thinking, right now. Behave.

Back to what's happening here. I rest my head on the pillow beside her. She half opens her eyes; she smiles and then closes her eyes again. My forehead touches her temple and I lay my arm on top of the duvet, across her chest. Taking hold of her PJ clad shoulder, which is peeping out over the top of the bedclothes; I pull her nearer to me. The deepness of her breathing tells me she's drifting into a peaceful sleep.

There's no viral infection at work here, this is evil at work. Poor Suzie, she didn't even ask about drama class.

"God bless you, Suzie. God will never desert you. He's watching over you," I whisper. There's a gentle knock on the bedroom door, and the door opens. Paul pops his head in. He's kind of taken aback when he sees me lying on the bed beside Suzie.

"Oh, sorry. I, I, I'll come back later," he says, nervously and he starts to close the door. Suzie stirs gently, but she doesn't wake up.

"No, Paul come on in," I say in a loud whisper, if that's possible. I lift my arm gently away from the sleeping beauty and I kiss her on the cheek. I slide off the bed and I go over to Paul, who's looking slightly uneasy. "Come on in big boy, she'll be glad to see you. She was just saying earlier how much she had missed seeing you today." I grab him by the wrist.

"Did she? But, you and she were… " His voice breaks off.

"There's no me and she doing anything. Go on, sit beside her. She's feeling down, she needs someone to hold her hand and you're the very guy. Go on now, I'll catch up with you later." I give Paul a friendly push and he grins at me. I watch him tiptoe across the room and he sits down gingerly on the edge of the bed.

"Paul, I'm so glad you're here. Can I snuggle in? I'm awfully beat." Suzie opens her eyes.

"Of course you can." My big friend's face lights up and Suzie rests her head onto his chest. I can see Paul isn't so sure what to do next, but these things come naturally and he's now stroking her dark hair. Her eyes are tightly closed. I can see she feels real safe in Paul's hands. I grab my shoes and slip out of the room quietly. She was kissed by a frog and got her prince I think. She won't notice I'm gone. But I'm not planning to vanish from Earth right at this moment, although others may have a different plan, so stay with me.

Chapter Twenty-Eight

With the LORD is unfailing love and with him is full redemption.

Psalm 130:7

I told you earlier about Jenny being very detached from what happened over at Apache Park, her whole emotional state was very out of character. It could be that her feelings towards me have cooled, fair enough, but why isn't she interested in Suzie? I need to try and find out what's going on. On leaving Suzie's place, I called Jen on her cell phone and I've arranged to meet her.

She had no qualms about meeting up and she suggested that we meet in Chaparral Park. She explained that as she's looking after her Aunt's dog, that location would be ideal. The park has off-leash areas, as well as being a real nice place to hang out. I asked her if Kushi was coming too, but it seems not. It seems that Kushi is still out of favor with Jenny. Thank you God. Two dogs. Eek!

One dog at a time is enough for me to cope with. Dogs aren't something I've had a lot of experience with since my arrival on Earth. So let's pray that me and this little doggy become real good buddies. Just in case the dog isn't too keen on angelets, I popped into the drugstore to buy it some treats. There's nothing like a bit of extra insurance, or should I say reassurance?

§ § §

Wow, did I say little doggy, earlier? Sorry, I should have said gi-normous hound. Calling him a doggy gives the impression that he's a cute, cuddly little thing that you can pop under your arm and I think he might take offense to that notion.

To pop this dog under your arm, you would require biceps similar to those of Dr. Bruce Banner when he changes into the Incredible Hulk. Let me draw a picture for your mind. This doggy resembles a mule whose head has been replaced with a rhino's, minus the horn. This dog is no Chihuahua.

I should have gone to the butchers for his treat, as a T-bone would undeniably be more appropriate. Got the picture firmly in place in that little pea brain of yours? I've broken out into a cold sweat, hope the deodorant plans to work overtime. They say that dogs can smell fear and at present, I'm humming with fear.

I'm grinning from ear to ear in an effort to fool this big guy and of course Jenny; after all I wouldn't like her to think I was some sort of wimp.

"Hi Jen. Who's this cute guy?" Okay, I lied. Smile, smile.

"This is Beelzebub."

I attempt to pat the top of his head, but I'm stopped in my tracks as he growls repeatedly and I can tell you the, Grrs, coming from this guy are fearsome. Note how I use a capital G in my description of the noise he's making. Gulp, gulp, I also gulped with a capital G.

"Oh, he probably just needs to get acquainted with me. It's a trust thing with animals." I'm flannelling with fear.

"He's normally very placid; his name is no reflection of his nature, I can assure you. I don't know what's gotten into him." Jenny tightens her grip on the devil dog as he's pulling on his leash. "Come on Beelzebub, Dan's a friend, behave. He won't throw your Frisbee to you if you don't, will you Dan?" she says playfully to big Beelze.

"Beelzebub and I are going to be great friends I'm

sure," I say with confidence. Beelze isn't so sure, he's flashing his gnashers at me. Saliva has started to foam around his lips and the droplets are falling onto the pathway. Ugh.

"What breed of dog is he?" As if I really want to know.

"He's an English Mastiff."

"I don't think I've seen one up close before." And it's not something I was planning. "Well, let's go and throw the Frisbee, pup." I speak to the dog playfully and the three of us start to walk over to the off leash area. Beelze has cooled his jets and is walking obediently beside Jen. "I went over to see Suzie earlier." I'm hoping to stir a response of concern.

"How is she?"

"She's wondering where her BFF is, that's for sure."

"Oh, I've had my hands full with this one here." She tugs at the dog's leash in a pretense of restraining him.

"You haven't taken the huff with her for any reason?"

"No, don't be ridiculous, what reason would I have? You've been with us most of the time."

"Hey, I'm not privy to all you girl's little secrets."

"You are."

"Girls have conversations that they don't share with male friends, just as us dudes don't tell you girls everything either."

"Give me an example."

"Well you'll speak about music, books, and eh, the dudes you think are hot in the movies. Eh, and waxing."

"Waxing?"

"Heck, I have no idea what girls talk about, I'm just guessing."

"What do you talk to Paul about then?"

"This and that. Eh, we speak about some of the awesome books we've read. Like 'A Farewell to Arms', for instance. And I love talking about Rock music, you must know that. Eh, and soccer of course, although Paul quickly changes the subject when I bring the subject of soccer up. Jenny you know some of this already, I'm sure."

Have you ever thought you've dug yourself into a hole and it's unlikely you're going to get out of it unscathed? Duh, I'm your guy.

"Do you ever talk about the movie stars, or the girls you think are hot?" asks Jenny. She's turned the tables on me. I was the guy that was trying to get to the bottom of the problem the girls seem to have. But I'm the guy that's now feeling the pressure. I think I know where this is going. Oh, ho…!

"I'm not really into movies. Therefore I don't have any idols of sorts. In fact I can't even think of one female movie stars name, off the top of my head," I say, cooly.

"Forget the movie stars then, Dan. Do you talk to Paul, about the girls you think are hot?"

"Jenny, I don't have the hots for any girl. I have love to give to two girls, and they're called Jenny and Suzie. Oh, and I love Aunt Sylvia of course, but in an aunty, nephew way. If you understand what I'm saying." This moment is real awkward. I don't really know what to say, to soothe her feelings. I want to hug her, but Beelze does that growling thing again, and of course I don't know how she would construe a hug.

"That's what I was afraid you would say," says Jenny despondently.

"Is that what this is all about? You're jealous that I have feelings for both you and Suzie?"

"Feelings, I don't really like that word. It's nondescript, it doesn't actually describe how you really feel about me.

Does it?"

"Jenny, I love you. But only as a friend. Anything else, I can't give you. I'm sorry."

"Oh Dan; you're impossible. When we were in drama class and I was playing Catherine, it all seemed so heartfelt. You meant those words you said to me, just as I meant every word I said to you. Those words of love were meant for us. No one else."

"Jenny, don't waste your love on me. I won't always be around."

"Why won't you be around?"

"Eh, eh, because eventually, I'll go to college, you'll go to college, we'll go our separate ways and that's what happens in the adult world. But the friendship you girls have is much deeper, it will survive the trials and tribulations of adulthood. Suzie will be your crutch when you shed tears for whatever reason and you'll be hers."

Beelze suddenly growls loudly at me, okay he's sussed out that I'm fibbing. I can hardly say I'm an angelet and I'll vanish from your life sometime in the very near future. Can I? I am telling the truth about us going our different ways though.

"I'll call over and see her tomorrow if she's not back at school, if that's what you want. As far as me shedding tears; if you think I'm going to shed any tears over you Dan Pierce, get over yourself," says Jenny huffily.

"That's my girl. Let's get throwing that Frisbee." At the mention of the Frisbee, Beelze's ears have popped up.

"Grrr, grrr." Beelze right on cue.

I open the gate of the doggy area and Jenny starts to take Beelze's leash off. I'm preparing myself for this dog to head straight for me once he's unleashed. Therefore I take one of the doggy treats out in anticipation.

Yep, here he comes. But surprise, surprise he isn't growling; he's started to lick the hand the snack is concealed in. Re-sult. He takes it greedily from me and sniffs about my person in search for other little tidbits. Mmm, I don't keep doggy treats in there. I slip my hand into my pocket and give him one more; bribery and corruption is the name of the game here.

"Good, you're Dan's friend now, Beelzebub. Let's play." Jenny throws the toy and Beelze watches it go. He opens his mouth and his large tongue protrudes from his black muzzle, showing the pink fleshy inner of his mouth and of course those ugly molars he uses for grinding his food. He pants as he ambles towards the plastic disc and a trail of saliva falls like dew on to the grass.

Jenny and I sit down at one of the picnic tables. Beelze looks back at us, but then walks slowly on to retrieve his beloved flying saucer.

"Jen, have you got over Kurt completely?"

"Yes, I have. Why do you ask?"

"You seemed to be concerned about the injury he got at soccer. You see, I reckon if you were truly over him, you wouldn't have reacted the way you did."

"You're being ridiculous." Her face reddens and she's avoiding looking me in the eye. "A lot of things went on between Kurt and I, Dan. We shared things, some very intimate and some I'm not proud of. At one time we were inseparable. That was until you came along. So maybe it's understandable that I have a slight soft spot for him."

"I get the point you're making. But, Jen, I can hear regret in your voice. You shouldn't regret breaking up with him, because he was no good for you. You say that you've shared things that you're not proud of, it's never too late to redeem yourself."

"Dan, spare me the sermon, you're starting to sound like my mom."

"I thought you and your mom were good now."

"We are. Listen, change the subject." Jen is not amused. Wow, I'm not either, because Beelze now has a spring in his step and is running towards me at a great rate of knots.

"Aaagh, aaagh." I'm lying on the ground. Beelze has just head butted me straight in the chest. I wish I had brought that T-bone with me.

Chapter Twenty-Nine

God is within her, she will not fall; God will help her at break of day.

Psalm 46:5

I needed some divine intervention to stop Beelze having me as his munchies. I managed to hypnotize him of sorts, using my special powers. When his senses were dulled I got him back on his leash and he was pretty docile for the walk back. Hopefully Jenny suspected nada. I'm not sure what's going on with Jen's Aunt's dog, but it is no normal pooch. No sir.

It crossed my mind that it was Isais doing his shape-shifter thing, but why would he all of a sudden decide to destroy me. I believe Beelze has some link to the Red Rider. I can say with some certainty that Beelze and I are going to meet up again.

School was pretty boring today, no drama class, no soccer. Math and English lit took up most of the day. Suzie is still stuck in bed, her mom says she's still no better. I was going to see her, but Jenny said she was going over with Paul. I decided that after Jen's tantrums yesterday, I would avoid going to Suzie's at the same time as her. I might try and visit later, in my spiritual state that is, while she sleeps.

Hopefully Jenny will see that a romance is blossoming between Paul and her BFF and stop being jealous. Right now, I'm sitting in the drugstore waiting on Paul. I've just finished an ice-cream soda float. Yummmy. Forgive me because the bubbles in the soda seemed to have left me with a little gas. Let's hope I don't do anything childish in public.

Here comes my big buddy and his facial expression tells me that something's worrying him. He sits down on the stool next to me.

"You look like the cat that got the cream," he says, surprisingly cheerfully.

"No, I was the cat that got the biggest ice-cream soda float you've ever seen."

"You're a glutton."

"You're jealous because you didn't have one."

"I'm not. In fact I'm really not too hungry. Suzie's mom gave me a slice of pie and a strawberry milkshake."

"I might have known you had some munchies, otherwise your order would have been in by now. How's Suzie?"

"She's real sick, Dan. I think she's worse than yesterday. The doc's still doing tests." Paul's initial cheery demeanor has all but disappeared.

"Didn't she cheer up when her BFF dropped by?"

"Jenny didn't turn up. She called Suzie on her cell phone and said that she had lots of homework to do. She was stressed out, so she couldn't make it over. Suzie became pretty distressed. But once she snuggled into me she calmed down."

"Snuggled up, did you? You devil you." Maybe I should rephrase that. Oh, what the heck.

"Don't tease Dan. I like Suzie a lot. But she's kind of fickle, isn't she?"

"What do you mean?"

"Well last week she was pledging her undying love for you, this week it could be me. Who will it be next week?"

"Listen big boy, sure at present she's appreciative of your bedside manner. But once she's up and about, you two will get to know each other and your love will blossom."

"Do you think so Dan?"

"I don't just think, I know."

§ § §

I'm standing on Isais's front porch and I've just rang the doorbell. Things are troubling me and I think I need to confront them head on. Pray that a werewolf, bear, or buzzard doesn't answer the door. Or, even Beelzebub.

The door opens. "Come in young Dan, what can I do for you?" says Isais smiling.

"It's kind of delicate and I hope you don't take offense at what I'm about to ask you." I follow Isais into his kitchen.

"Sounds rather ominous boy. Sit down, can I get you soda, or a root beer?"

"No, nada, I've had my fill of soda tonight."

"So what do you want to ask me?"

"Why did you kill JoJo?"

"Well young un', there was no delicate way to put that, was there?"

"No, but it's a straight forward question."

"She had to be destroyed, Dan."

"But why did you take it upon yourself to kill her?"

"Dan, she wasn't a human being, just as you aren't, just as Sylvie isn't. She was a fallen angel, an angel of Satan. A demon."

"Are you human?"

"Yes, I told you I'm a skin-walker. I'm a human with supernatural powers."

"I don't know why you are getting involved in this whole angel and demon thing. Surely you have enough evil things to be getting on with."

"Is that what you think of me, Dan? Evil?"

"I don't want to think of you being evil. But if you go about killing, what else can I believe?"

"Dan, if I hadn't destroyed her she would have destroyed you and anyone else that might represent good. She had to be stopped. She would have continued recruiting young uns' like Kurt and his friends. Priming them for the Devil to possess their souls. Making the world a very dangerous place."

"What's in it for you?"

"I have my reasons Dan. Believe me, I have my reasons."

"I read recently that a skin-walker's initiation involves killing a close male member of their family. Did you kill someone close to you?"

"My gift was passed down to me by my forefathers. In their struggles with the army, they had to change their appearance so they could evade capture and persecution."

"You didn't answer my question. If you killed JoJo you probably did kill a relative."

"I didn't kill her, I'm no murderer. She was an evil spirit. I destroyed her. She is no longer any use to her master. Good has to overcome evil, Dan. Otherwise Satan will take over this world and maybe even yours."

"Isais, I don't know what to make of you."

"I'm asking you to trust me, because young un' you need my help."

"Maybe I do." What choice do I have? I haven't always been on the winning side recently. "I need to ask you this: did you shape-shift into an English Mastiff today by any chance?"

"No I didn't, why?"

"Jenny has a new dog friend called Beelzebub and I'm kind of suspicious."

"Good job you've got a skin-walker for a friend then."

§ § §

"Dan, Suzie's in the hospital. She's been admitted to Osborn. Pop brought me over. She's in a coma." Paul's called me from his cell and he sounds frantic.

"I'll get Isais to bring me over immediately. Don't worry big buddy." I press the end call button on my cell.

My bedroom door opens and in comes Aunt Sylvia. "You must go and sit with her, Dan. Just remember: God is with you both." She hugs me.

"I'm going to ask Isais to take me over, do you have any objections?"

"It's not my place to object Dan. You're doing the right thing by going to the hospital, and that's all I will say." Aunt Sylvia's reply in relation to Isais is as clear as used dish-water. But I've made my decision, I'm asking Isais to go with me to the hospital. I'll know when I'm smoldering in that great sulfur lake that I made the wrong move.

Chapter Thirty

Do not be afraid of what you are about to suffer. I tell you, the devil will put some of you in prison to test you, and you will suffer persecution for ten days.

Revelation 2:10

"Hey big boy, how is she?" The sound of my voice startles Paul. I've found him sitting in the waiting area of the ICU. When I first saw him he was slouched over and staring down into his clasped hands. I don't know if he was praying, or just looking for answers? God only knows.

"Hi Dan, thank goodness you're here. Her mom and dad are with the doc at present. She's on a life support machine. Dan, she's going to die, I know she is." Paul starts to weep. I put my arm around his wide shoulders, his body shakes with silent sobs. I give him the biggest bear hug ever. He pulls himself together and wipes his face with the back of one of his large hands. His tears smear over his face, leaving wet tracks down his now ruddy cheeks.

"Oh heck, are things that bad?" Isais has appeared, he'd been parking his truck.

"Her parents are with the doc." I can still feel Paul's body shake with his sorrow. I keep my arm around his shoulders as I relay the news. Isais sits down on the chair on the other side of Paul and pats him on the knee reassuringly.

"Listen boy, I've heard that this is one of the best hospitals in Scottsdale. In fact in Arizona. These docs know what they're about."

"Paul, come on. You're no use to her if you fall apart,"

I say.

"Okay, I'm acting like a cry baby. But I've never felt so positive about my life, in a long time." He bites his bottom lip and shakes his head in disillusionment.

"That could change at any time." The sound of Kurt's voice causes the three of us to look up in astonishment. He and Jenny are standing in the open doorway and he's got a real superior look on his face. A rather concerned looking Jenny walks forward.

"I called Kurt because he's one of Suzie's friends too. His mom brought us over," she says tensely. "My mom wasn't home. I didn't know who else to call. Your Aunt Sylvia told me that you had already left."

My heart has suddenly been ripped from my chest and is bouncing across the floor. Okay, I'm exaggerating and that hasn't literally happened, but I feel as though it has. It's difficult for me to put in words how I feel right now. I'm dumbfounded; I love the word dumfounded, make it your word of the day. Right now, it's without a doubt my word for the day.

Paul's face was pale before, but he's now as white as a sheet. Isais stares at the pair of new arrivals.

"I'm sure Suzie and her family will appreciate the support. We're just waiting on news," says Isais convincingly. He should have joined the diplomatic core.

He could be sent as a State department envoy to some far off land. Why? Because he's certainly dealing with this more than unexpected situation more tactfully than I could. Jenny sits down beside me. Kurt is still hanging around the doorway like the distinct odor of parfum de rat.

"Can I get anyone coffee?" says Kurt amicably.

Paul, Isais, and I make negative grunting sounds, but none of us actually speak.

"I would like a soda Kurt, thanks," says Jenny.

We three amigos watch Kurt as he about turns and exits the room.

"I can't believe you brought him here Jen," I say.

"Is that the green-eyed monster I'm seeing Dan?" says Jenny haughtily.

"Why does it always have to be about you, Jen? Don't answer that; we can have this discussion another time." She's made me really mad.

But it seems that I'm not the only one who's feeling a little annoyed, Jenny's face is flushed. Paul and Isais look rather bemused at my outburst. Jenny doesn't have time to reply, because Suzie's mom and dad have come into the room.

"Thanks, kids, for coming," says Mr. Kowalski. "And?" he looks at Isais questioningly.

"My name's Isais Bia. I'm young Dan's neighbor. I've met your daughter several times, she's a good kid. I came to help support the boys here."

"Well, thank you Isais, for your kindness," says Suzie's dad. "At present the doc has no idea what's wrong with Suzie. He explained to us that her vitals are weak and that her system may have gone into shutdown. In order that it can try to heal itself. He still thinks it's some kind of viral infection."

"So, is there nothing they can do for her?" asks Isais.

"They're pumping her with antibiotics hoping that she'll start to show some improvement. He also thinks that it would be good if ourselves and you kids speak to her in turns. It may stimulate her brain. After all, she may be able to hear us and she just can't respond," says Mr. Kowalski hopefully.

"We've spent quite a bit of time with her already, so we would very much appreciate if maybe Dan and Paul could sit with her for a while. I know you two boys make her laugh," says her mom warmly.

I don't know if it's my imagination, but I could swear that Mrs. Kowalski keeps looking at me rather oddly.

"Of course we will Mrs. Kowalski. Come on Dan," says Paul eagerly as he stands up and starts to pull me to my feet.

We pass Kurt on our way out, he's coming back into the room carrying coffees.

"Jenny will fill you in, Kurt," I say amiably. I'm becoming rather good at being two-faced. Sorry God.

A flash of purple shows itself on Kurt's face, but he quickly controls his devilish traits and is very human looking.

"Sure thing Dan. Good luck." His words make me feel physically sick. Hey, but no time to vomit, I need to see Suzie.

§ § §

"Dan, hold on for a minute," I hear a woman call after me. Turning around I see it's Mrs. Kowalski, following us hurriedly along the corridor.

"You go on and gown up. I'll catch up with you in a moment," I say to Paul. Looking kind of mystified, Paul leaves me. Mrs. Kowalski, having now caught up with us, waits until Paul is out of earshot.

"You're not here to take her away are you?" she says. Well blow me down, what the heck is she talking about?

"I'm here as a friend Mrs. Kowalski," I say innocently.

"I know you're from the spirit world, please don't take her from us." This woman is seriously spooky.

"Ma'am, I'm not taking Suzie anywhere that I know of. Maybe you should go and get some rest. You're going to need every bit of strength you can muster. We'll come and get you if there's any change." I take hold of her hand and stroke it lightly. The middle-aged woman has her eyes transfixed on my face.

"I'm sorry, I don't know what got into me. Of course you're a good friend to her. Yes, come and get us. Thanks, for being here." She turns and leaves me standing, dumfounded. I knew I'd have reason to use our word of the day, again.

§ § §

Paul and I have been sitting with Suzie for just over an hour. I've been talking about our parts in the play and Paul has been reminiscing about some of the fun times we've had in recent months. There are tubes sticking out of her all over the place. The ventilator makes a strange swooshing sound as it compresses the air that's being delivered to her through a breathing tube into her throat. I don't really understand the full ins and outs of it to explain it you. But hey, I'm an angelet not a doctor.

The heart and blood monitors that are attached to her by small pads *beep, beep, beep*. She looks mighty helpless lying there. We watch her attentively, just in case an eye-lid flickers, or a muscle contracts. But nothing. God bless her and watch over her. I hope the man upstairs is listening to me today.

"Do you two want to take some time out?" Jenny has tiptoed in. I don't want to be angry with her, because she's so gor… You can finish the word. The door opens behind her and in comes Kurt.

"No way," says Paul defiantly.

"Don't worry, we'll take care of her," says Kurt. He has that arrogant grin on his face, that's now sooo familiar. But at least he's not purple.

"Come on Paul, say goodbye, we can come back later. Jenny and Suzie have been friends for a long time. They can talk about chick things." I stand up and I tug at his arm. I am hesitant about leaving Suzie with them, but I'm uncertain what to do. I kiss her forehead and step aside to let Paul in to say his farewell. He kisses her tenderly on the cheek and the two of us head for the door. If looks could kill, Kurt would be dead. Paul has just given him a dagger of a glance.

"We will look after her," says Jenny. I can hear a note of concern in her voice.

We have no option but to leave Suzie with them.

§ § §

To pass the time Isais has suggested we go grab a bite to eat. It's midnight and the hospital restaurant is fairly quiet. I can't say I feel too hungry, but I might as well snack. Don't you agree? Do you know sometimes you're very, very opinionated?

I've suddenly been overcome by a very, very strange sensation. Pictures are flashing chaotically into my mind. I can see Suzie fighting with something, I'm not sure what the creature is. It's accompanied by one of those purple kids. Whoa, I feel real woozy and confused.

"We need to go to Suzie," says Isais in my ear. Paul's ahead of us in the line and he's busily filling his coffee cup; hopefully he won't notice we're gone.

Isais and I rush along the corridor to the elevator. He can half sprint for a big guy. *Ting,* the elevator doors open, we both jump in and I press number three on the panel. The doors seem to shut so slowly. We start to move, *chung, chung, chung, ting,* we're here. The doors start to slide open, Isais and I prime ourselves for our next dash.

"Wah-wee, whoa." That's me exclaiming my horror at what has just leapt towards the lift doors. The welcoming committee comes in the shape of huge version of Beelze. This guy must be his pop. His gaping mouth fills the entrance, wow, it's a cavern. If I had known I was going to be faced with this, I'd have brought a miners lamp.

I'm now gawping at teeth, which resemble huge sabers, and a large red coiling tongue that's sloshing about. Yuck. I thank God for small mercies, because Papa B's head is too big to get into the cabin. But the big wiggly thing that's moving in and out of his mouth could be a problem, without a doubt.

As I step back, my foot hits something solid. Isais must be behind me. But I daren't look back, as I can't lose sight of Papa B. I quickly step to the side and start to move backwards, ducking and diving, bobbing and a weaving, to miss the tongue. I really don't want to French kiss this guy. I'm aiming for the far left corner; Papa B's tongue can't quite reach there.

Whoa, whoa, there's a strange creature in the elevator beside me. He's a big stripy lizard type; I think he's some kind of gigantic Gila Monster. His tongue is darting in and out of his mouth too, but thankfully he's not aiming at me. If he carries on like this, he'll end up playing a game of tonsil hockey with Papa B.

My back's against the wall now and I'm now out of my attacker's way. I grab hold of the steel rail to steady myself, because this cabin is now doing quite a bit of rattling and rolling. I quickly look around and take stock of my dangerous surroundings. Isais is nowhere to be seen; he must have shape shifted into this big scaly monster.

As Scaly steps slowly forward, his heavy steps cause the elevator floor to vibrate. Papa B retreats slightly as his opponent continues to progress forward, but Papa B isn't going to give up, he wants me more than anything. He lunges forward forcing his head against the entryway and the elevator shudders. The cables and brakes are under real strain. I hope I'm not going to plummet into the great depths below. No, not hell; but the basement of this building. Wow, he misses me again.

But Scaly will never be called Wimpy, because he's one brave dude. Papa B withdraws and closes his mouth, causing saliva to dribble from the sides. If he carries on like this, I'll need a life jacket. Imagine drowning in a sea of spittle. Yuck. No pictures please.

Scaly seizes an opportunity, he takes hold of Papa B's throat with his grooved teeth and bites into the soft flesh. The demon yelps; he sounds like a Pekinese that's been trod on. There's a greenish liquid starting to ooze out of Scaly's mouth. Whoa, does that liquid smell; it's worse than Papa B's breath. I can say that Scaly definitely has halitosis.

Scaly keeps a grip of Papa B, who appears to be growing weaker and weaker. He's no longer putting up a fight, he's shrinking, smaller and smaller. The head, the body, shrink, shrink. His form is now changing, it's changing into the shape of a human.

OMG, Papa B has changed into Robbie. He's still shrinking, and one thing you can say is, he's never been no violet. He's now miniscule, plop, he's vanished. Oh, oh, Scaly is starting to change. I'm having a mild attack of vertigo, just watching the transformation.

Isais is now standing beside me, he puts what looks like a reptile skin purse into his pocket.

"I'm sorry I had to do that," he says.

"He was always an insignificant little twerp anyway." I shake my head in incredulity. Isais has had to kill again to save my neck, this can't be right.

Chapter Thirty-One

"Do not be afraid, Daniel. Since the first day that you set your mind to gain understanding and to humble yourself before your God, your words were heard, and I have come in response to them."

Daniel 10:12

Everything is real weird and for the first time I'm absolutely crapping myself. Sorry, that language was a bit out of line. I'll be struck down by a bolt of lightning at any time. Hard hats to the ready. Brace myself, brace position adopted. Hold.

Nope, no mysterious weather conditions in Scottsdale at present. But I used the slang terminology, cra…, no I'm not going to chance my luck and say it again. I needed a good descriptive verb to explain how I'm feeling right now and that one popped into my head. Very un-angel like indeed.

Following the destruction of Papa B, Isais and I went charging along the corridor like two bulls in a china shop. But in that instance, the two bulls were headed for room 345. Images of destruction kept flashing in and out of my mind. The destruction of Suzie to be blunt. But as I don't have a lot of experience in reading these images, I wasn't sure as to the accuracy of my interpretation. But Isais also believed she was in danger and so far his instincts have been spot on. So we charged on, like the cavalry.

Isais and I arrived at room 345 and burst in through the door to rescue our damsel in distress. To our astonishment, we only found a doctor and a nurse standing over Suzie. They were doing one thing or another with the monitors and tubes, nothing suspicious. But no sign of Jen, or parfum de rat. The stern nurse looked at us with venom in her eyes and she said, "Shhh. Get out."

Well, we didn't hang around. It wouldn't have been a very clever idea to provoke this woman. We were, yes, dumfounded at what we found. Both of us had acted like a pair of fools, barging on in there like that. But we were left with the question: where were Jenny and Kurt?

Enigma solved, we've walked back into the restaurant and the cozy couple are sitting together in a cozy corner. Thank God they haven't moved in on Paul.

"Go sit with Paul, I'll grab us some food," says Isais. He puts a finger to his lips to stop me from answering him. "Go, he'll think you've been with him all the time. Trust me."

I move over to where Paul's sitting and quickly sit down opposite him, he stops eating and looks at me very strangely. You know that look, there's a light on, but no-one's actually at home. Snap, the switch is clicked to on in Paul's brain. He's back.

"You not hungry?" he asks.

"Isais is grabbing me a bite."

"Good, because I'm not sharing mine." He resumes tucking into his plate of macaroni and cheese. Still eating, Paul looks up from his plate and his eyes wander around the room. I know by the expression on his face that he's caught sight of Jenny and Kurt. He stops munching and he says, "Have you seen who's over there?"

"Yes, it's cool."

"He's going to reclaim your girl's heart, Dan."

"She's not my girl, she's her own girl."

"Come on, I've seen the way you look at her; the way she looks at you. You've tried not to get involved, your excuse being because of school commitments. But it can't be all work and no play. Go for it buddy."

"Paul, Jenny and I will never get together. I mean

never."

Before Paul can add anything, Isais arrives with a full tray of food. Thank God, maybe Paul will change the subject. I'm not cool about Jenny and Kurt's renewed friendship. But I don't know if it's because of my feelings for her, or because I should be protecting her from the disciple of the Red Rider. Then love does make you protective, doesn't it?

If jealousy is my problem, I deserve everything I get, even if that means being submerged in the burning river of sulfur. Paul's still glancing across the room surreptitiously at the pair.

"Why's Jenny not with Suzie?" asks Paul inquisitively.

"The medical staff needed some time with her," answers Isais without any hesitation.

"Nothing's wrong is it?" Paul looks troubled.

"No, the nursing staff just need to get her freshened up and record her vitals. That's how they can work out if she's responding to treatment or not," says Isais informatively.

"Sure; I'm going to go back after I've finished here. Are you coming, Dan?" Paul's mind has been put at ease.

"Try and stop me," I say keenly.

Oh, what? A very strange image has flashed into my head. If what I'm seeing was on a TV screen, I'd be adjusting the brightness control. I can see a woman holding a babe in arms. The baby's crying, she rocks the infant back and forth. The baby stops crying and starts to gurgle. The woman smiles, a kind smile, a warm smile, a mother's smile. She kisses the child on top of the head. I can feel the warmth of the kiss. That woman is no ordinary woman, she's my mom.

"Dan, are you okay boy?" The sound of Isais's voice startles me.

"Yes, I'm just a bit tired. It's been a long day." I pretend to yawn.

"Yes, it has. I think you boys should go and say your goodbyes to Suzie and get home for some sleep. You've both got school to go to."

"I think I'll just stay here. I can catch up with my school work another time," says Paul.

"Boy, I assured your pop that I'd look after you and it's no use you two kids exhausting yourselves. Listen, how about a compromise? I'll take you both home, but I'll return and sit for another couple of hours. If there's any change in her, good or bad, I'll come and get you both. Deal?" Isais looks from Paul to me for our acceptance of his suggestion.

"Deal." Paul forces a smile.

"Dan?" asks Isais.

My head's all over the place. I want to stay, because I fear for Suzie's well-being. But I can't concentrate. I'm confused. Was the vision I just had a glimpse of the real me?

"Yes, as always you're right Isais." I nod in agreement. I think it would be for the best, I need to clear my head.

Isais doesn't respond to me, he's looking across the room towards Kurt and Jenny.

"Jenny's coming over boys. Smile," he says.

I feel Jenny's presence, she touches my shoulder and my body tingles from head to toe. A passage from the Bible, Genesis to be exact, pops into my head; Adam, Eve, and the serpent features. I'm sure you've read it, or at least you've heard about it.

"Kurt's going home, can I hang out with you guys?" She looks at each of us in turn, in search of a response.

"We're not going to stay much longer. Suzie's mum and dad will be back soon; then we're going to shoot.

Paul's staying at his gran's, so it would be kind of out of our way. Maybe you'd be better getting a ride home with Kurt," I say snappily.

"I'd rather stay and get a lift home with you, Dan." Her eyes are pleading with me.

"If it's cool with Paul and Isais, it'll be cool with me," I say weakly. I could kick myself for giving in to her. Both Paul and Isais nod, so it looks like Jen's coming home with us.

"I'll go tell Kurt," says Jenny.

I turn around and watch her go to him. Their body language isn't giving much away, other than he really has the hots for her. But her face is expressionless.

"I can't work out what's going on between those two, can you Dan?" asks Paul.

"I can't either. One minute she hates him, the next he's her BFF," I say sounding flummoxed.

"Boy, never try to understand women, they're very complex creatures. I can tell you on very good authority," says Isais jovially and then he laughs loudly. Good old Isais, he always manages to lighten the mood with some words of wisdom.

§ § §

Paul was dropped off first at his Gran's and Jenny insisted that she get off at my house. Isais has reluctantly obliged; which means, yes, I'm walking her home.

"When I see poor Suzie lying in hospital, it makes me think about my own mortality. How about you Dan?" asks Jenny. She takes hold of my arm and cozies in.

Gulp, gulp. "I can't say I've really ever thought about it?" The lie just seems to trip off my tongue these days.

"Are you telling me that you've never questioned, in your own mind, as to how we came to be here, or where we go when we die?"

"I came to Arizona on a Greyhound bus and as to what happens to our spirits when we die, what's the point of surmising? We'll know when we get there."

"Don't be so flippant Dan."

"Jenny, I was brought up to believe in the teachings of the Holy Bible. So it has never occurred to me to believe anything other than the whole heaven and hell thing. Suzie's not going to die, Jenny. So stop being so morbid."

"You're right. I'm just being silly." She tightens her grip on my arm and puts her head on my shoulder. I want to put my arms around her, hold her close and kiss her real slow. Whoa, what am I saying? Whoa, pictures, pictures. It's that woman and a baby again. Is something, or someone, playing games inside my head? That's brought me back to reality. If being a celestial being on Earth could be called reality. Relax, we're outside Jenny's house.

"Goodnight Jenny, see you tomorrow. I'll call you if I receive any news about Suzie."

She puts her arms around my neck. Her nose touches my nose. The feelings I have charging through my body are electrifying. If I was human, they would say my hormones were raging.

I shouldn't have had an egg mayo baguette earlier, for munchies, it really stinks your breath. Be warned, all you budding Lotharios out there. What does it matter if my breath stinks? I'm not going to kiss her. She's pouting. Yes, she's pouting. She's pressing her body hard against mine. Hormones, hormones, hormones.

But hey, I'm one cool dude. I'm taking hold of her arms, I'm hesitating, oh, how I'm he-si-tating. She feels so nice. You're going to be so proud of me. Yes you are. I'm pulling her arms from around me and I pull my face back from hers. "I don't think this is very appropriate when our friend is lying ill in hospital, do you?" You're so proud of me. I bet your chest has puffed up with pride hasn't it? Don't deny it.

"I suppose not. Please give me a call if her condition changes. Otherwise I'll see you at school," says Jenny reluctantly.

"Yes I'll see you tomorrow." Taking a deep breath, I walk away from her. I have my regrets walking away, but I have to or…or what? Well I don't know, do I? Should I take the chance? I'm glad you said no. You did, didn't you?

Now let's start to puzzle out why I keep getting visions of a smiley woman and a child and of course there was the other strange vision of monsters tampering with Suzie. Puzzled, you should be. We can think about it together, on the walk home. If you come up with any bright ideas, make sure you tell me. But how likely is it that you'll have any bright ideas? Ha-ha. I'm just being a little devil. Not literally, needless to say.

I'll be home in ten minutes and I have to admit I'm beat. But before I can think about going to bed, I'm faced with the problem of Suzie's deteriorating state of health. I haven't been given any miracle powers, but I do have the power of prayer. But I won't bore you with the details. Amen.

Round the next corner is home, sweet, home. I might go and see Suzie later. Well, spiritually at least, not in human form as that's a bit more difficult. But I think I'll rest the whole of me for an hour or so. Isais will call if things change.

Oooh, I hate to tell you; I'm not going straight home. I have a slight problem. There's a purple guy, called Kurty, standing in front of me.

"Sss, sss." He's a noisy dude, isn't he? He lunges forward, the pointy bits on his tail just miss my head. I can tell you, my good looks would be seriously demolished if he had managed to catch me. I've just left my human form. Needs must, dangerous times ahead, no Isais here to save my butt.

"You had your chance, Dan. You had the chance to be a disciple. You chose not to take the path. Those who choose not to join Satan must be destroyed. This is the Red Riders world. He controls all our destinies," says Kurt with superiority.

"Hogwash, Kurt. He doesn't call the shots," I say defiantly. I try to spread my particles as far apart as possible. I'm trying to make it difficult for Kurt to see me, but he's getting to grips with my tactics.

Whoa did you see that? Sorry, of course you didn't. Trust me, his big pincer missed me by a hair length and I mean my human cropped hair length. He's doing that salivating thing. His tail arcs towards me, there's stuff dribbling from his mouth. A sticky brown liquid, oh, the smell. I bet you're glad this isn't a scratch and sniff book. He must have eaten a sardine sandwich earlier, but the filling must have been sitting in the sun for some time before it was consumed.

"You and your kind have to be destroyed," says Kurt in a gurgle.

"Who's going to destroy me, big boy? You? No way," I shout.

"I will destroy you," says Kurt viciously.

I need to go on the attack. I need to subdue him, take the sting out of his tail, so to speak. He's not used to me being the aggressor; I have to save myself. I feel force go through my body. Push forward, push forward, a red light emanates from my metaphorical arm and I zap my friend in his chest with force.

Holy cow, he's smashed onto the ground. I never knew I had that in me. That power came straight from the soles of my boots, or somewhere deep down in my spirit. I couldn't say for certain and I definitely don't have time to discuss it.

He struggles to get to his feet, but he manages. He tries to swipe me with his right pincer, but I find the power to hit him again and he lands on his behind. I'm not going to give him the chance to come back at me, so I go at him again.

"Eek," he squeals and I mean like a pig. He's hurt. I can see blood coming from his leg and that's good enough for me. I don't think he's fit to fight back. It's time to gather myself together and go home to Aunt Sylvia.

Whoosh, I'm back in my human form. I can tell you I'm ready for my bed now, let's go. Hold on, I want to have a word with my devilish amigo.

"You really do need to start using mouthwash, Kurt. It would get rid of that nasty smell of sardines from your breath." Ha, ha.

Chapter Thirty-Two

One of the heads of the beast seemed to have had a fatal wound, but the fatal wound had healed.

Revelation 13:3

Whirl, whirl, whirl, my head's in a whirl; my head is in a spin. It's not actually spinning on my shoulders, but it might as well be. I feel as though my emotions are like a runaway train, totally out of control, speeding along the track, sparks flying, ready to leave its meandering path at any point in time.

My angelic locomotive has the potential to hit a huge boulder with tremendous impact today. The boulder being drama class. I don't want you to breathe another word to anyone of what I'm about to tell you. I know you won't, but I've got so much to lose if you engage in loose-talk.

I'm admitting that I could leave the rails if I don't get a grip of my feelings. Do you know where I'm coming from? You have no idea how much I wanted Jenny last night, she just felt sooo good, she just smoldered in my arms. She smelt so sweet, and the tingling I felt rush through my body felt awesome.

If you thought that secret I've let you into is a heavy burden to carry, there's worse to come. I'm going to have to blurt this out, or it'll stick in my throat. I need to compose myself. Wait, don't be so impatient. I…I…I… I'm gathering myself together, okay. Ready, steady, go: I had the impulse to annihilate Kurt. Problem is I didn't and it's part of the job description. It's one urge I should have fulfilled. I can't expect Isais to do all my Devil slaying for me.

That other urge, you know that urge I had when I was with Jenny, come on you know, don't be thick. Good it's clicked; well that urge is a definite no go, non starter. The starting pistol can't even go off accidentally.

Now that I've got that off my chest, I feel better. Unlike Suzie, who's still on the critical list. Isais just called, there's no change in her condition. I managed to drift over last night. I held her hand and prayed. But I don't know if my prayers are falling on deaf ears.

Why did I just say that? Prayers never fall on deaf ears. Such negativity is definitely non productive and certainly not good for the soul. Positive thoughts, positive thoughts. Okay, I can confirm those negative feelings have now been put in a box and I've thrown away the key. Actually I've just put my imaginary key on a piece of string and put it around my neck. Hopefully I'll lose it later and I'll never be able to take my negativity back out of its flimsy container.

Suzie's mom is definitely tapped into the spirit world. She must have some kind of psychic powers. When I spirited in to see Suzie, her mom and pop were by her bedside. Mrs. K became uneasy when I arrived, she kept glancing around the room furtively in the likelihood that she would catch sight of the non physical being she sensed. She didn't make a big deal about her suspicions, because quite understandably she didn't want to upset her husband.

But she knew there was something spooky going down, that's for sure. She mentally tried to contact me, well she didn't know it was me. She was trying to contact my world and identify who her visitor from the spirit world was. But she'll need to get up early to catch me.

Another secret I need to let you into is that I really don't feel like going to school today. I would have liked a duvet day, but that isn't possible in my kind of work. It's not possible for you either if you want to get your grades. So don't even think about it. One consolation about going to school is that I can keep an eye on Kurt there and of course I can see Jen. There I go again, with my non angelic thoughts.

§ § §

Awesome, awesome, awesome. I wish you could have watched the movie with me. Oh sorry, you don't know what the heck I'm talking about, do you? Now pay attention for goodness sake. You really should go to bed earlier. All that listening to music until the wee small hours is turning your brain into mush.

Drama class, that's where I saw a movie, okay, you with me now? Miss Summerville was called away unexpectedly and she decided that it would be advantageous for us to watch a movie adaptation of 'A Farewell to Arms'. It was made in 1932, directed by a guy called Frank Borzage. The movie, like other movies, isn't completely true to the novel, but hey ho, it made tremendous watching. Fantastic.

Freddy was played by Gary Cooper and Cath was played by Helen Hayes. I prefer the names Freddy and Cath, because Frederic and Catherine sounds so formal. Using their formal names makes me think I'm talking to their moms all of the time.

You understand what I'm saying, don't you? I mean to say, we all have good friends that we have pet names for, but heck you wouldn't use their pet name in front of their mom. She would be totally offended, after all the name she gave your buddy was her choice. Get my meaning? Sorry, I'm off on a tangent again.

Anyway, panic over, there was actually no need for me to break out into a cold sweat over drama class. Because I didn't need to hold Jen in my arms and call her darrrling, or sweeetheart, or sausage. Where on earth did I get the endearment sausage from?

I think I've been staying up too late with you, listening to music and my brain has mushed into a great dollop of something, or another. Probably cream. No impudent comments from you required, just as no kissing is required, today anyway.

There definitely is no passsionate, full on the lipsss kissing required as an angelet, that's for sure. Notice how I stumble over some words, the words that get me in a real tizz, especially when Jen's involved in the same sentence.

Do you ever get into a tizzy when you see someone that you really, and I mean really fancy? Hey, that wasn't a confession from me. I was just asking you a question. Okay, no need to reply.

§ § §

To my many male friends out there, who are tagging along for the ride, there's a question I would like to put to you. Do you understand women? No, I thought not. They're a very strange species indeed. I apologize to my ardent, swooning female fans out there. But, girls, you do sometimes blow a little hot and cold don't you?

It's that old cliché 'she loves me, she loves me not, that is the question.' I know I should be holding some kind of a flower and pulling at the petals, but in Arizona I'd be likely to pick a cactus and oh do those spines cause some pain when you try to pull at them.

Who is the girl I'm talking about? Jen, of course. I think she's probably thrown the pacifier and dolly out of the pram, because of last night. Boy oh boy, is she cool towards me today. She's so cold; I thought I'd been transferred to Alaska, unbeknownst to me.

She's not walking home with Paul and I from school; she said she wants to do work in the library. Duh, really, do I look that dumb? Not a word from you. Not a word. She's never stayed behind to study in her life.

The result of her rejection of my wonderful company is that I'm just waiting on my lonesome, waiting for big boy. Do I hear you say, oh diddums? Thought so, you never let a moment pass without mocking me. You might also rebuff me when I tell you I wouldn't have time to gossip with you otherwise.

Look out here comes big boy. I grin, because I'm not too macho to admit I love my big buddy Paul.

"How you holding up neighbor?" I ask.

"Okay, but all the better for seeing your smiley face. Dan, you always look so happy, you're infectious." Paul slaps me on the back and I nearly fall over.

"Thanks for the compliment," I say coyly, as I do have some humility. At least I seem to be doing something right.

"It's a compliment that's honestly deserved," he says, genuinely. Big boy must be hungry, he's walking at a fair pace with me struggling to keep up.

"We'll go over to the hospital after dinner, okay?" I slap him on the back, but he doesn't even flinch.

"Okay," says Paul happily.

"Paul, I've forgotten something back in my locker. I'll need to go back."

"Oh, okay. I'll catch you later." Paul walks on. I haven't really forgotten anything, I have a little problem. OMG, do I have a problem. If you guess a purple monster is waiting for me, you've guessed wrong. There's a humungous tan colored locust blocking the sidewalk. Who's this guy? Aaaah, answer's by email.

"Chirrrp, chirrrp, chirrrp." Listen to the bugs call. I hope he's not calling in for back up from his swarm of friends. Swarm, get it, swarm, ohhh, forget it.

"Chirrrp, chirrrp, chirrrp." This must be his war cry, because he's coming towards me at top speed with his great wings flapping so hard that they're making a whirring sound. The antennae on top of his cone shaped head replicate long horns and I would think should be avoided at all costs. Oh and those eyes.

His eyes are on massive stalks sticking out from the side of his strange face. His golden locks blow in the wind created from his vibrating wings. Yes I did say golden locks, strange but true. I know all God's creatures are beautiful, but Lucifer's definitely fall short of that description. Whoa is he tall, he's standing up on his muscle bound hind legs. Whirrr, whirrr.

He leaps at me; *whoosh,* that's me transforming. He misses. I move behind him and I push light through my body. Push, I push with all my might. Out comes the light through the tips of my fingers and I hit my opponents crusty shell with force. He drops down onto all fours, at least I've made some impact.

I spoke too soon. He stands up again, his wings violently vibrate. He has no trouble seeing me, that's for certain. He uses his flapping wings to lift himself off the ground and ouch, that's me hitting the deck. He lands on top of me and he opens his mouth wide.

"Oh Grandma, what big teeth you have." I slither from beneath him and I leap to my feet. I knock him to the ground with forcing light again. His front leg snaps in two. Reeesult. There I go again, opening my big mouth. Miraculously his leg heals and he jumps at me. I swoop up into the air, missed.

God help me, gosh, a goat has appeared. Whose side is this guy on? Not to worry, he's just butted Loco up into the air. He's on my side. Loco's wing breaks, again some kind of magical healing takes place. He's coming for me, aaargh, I've been decked again. No time to check if I've been injured or not. I go at him again with light. I push him towards the goat and he butts Loco's butt, who in turn goes straight up into the air.

He's vanished into thin air, where did Loco go? The goat looks around, he bends his front legs at the knees and takes a bow. Heck, I can't thank him, he's gone, poof, just like a puff of smoke.

Chapter Thirty-Three

Dear friends, do not believe every spirit, but test the spirits to see whether they are from God, because many false prophets have gone out into the world.

1 John 4:1

"I'm starting to think that I'm not cut out for this type of work. Since arriving here on earth, what have I actually achieved?" I'm so filled with self doubt, I think maybe it's time to throw in the towel.

"Boy, why are you coming over all morose? Where's that bubbly, self-assured character I've grown to know and love?" Isais puts his big arm around me and gives me a reassuring hug. He hugs me so tight, I get that crushed organ feeling again.

"I think the guy you know has shape shifted and turned into a silly goat like you did earlier."

We've just got home after visiting Suzie, where the doctors are talking about turning off her life support. So as you can imagine it's kind of hard to be optimistic. I thanked Isais earlier for his agile intervention, but as usual he makes no big deal out of it.

I stab at the margherita pizza on my plate and pull at the stringy mozzarella with my fork. I have no inclination to even attempt to eat it. You know by now that if I'm not ready to munch, I have a problem. The problem I have, not even Houston could help me with. I feel sick; sick to the core, sick with worry, sick with fear of the unknown.

"Dan, the way I see it, you have achieved many things since your arrival. I can't tell you if your achievements are of the quality you need to gain entry into heaven. But I think in anyone's book you have done a lot of good and

I'm sure that will be recognized." Isais is trying hard to set my mind at rest.

"What have I achieved?" I'm full of pessimism.

"Well, there's young Paul for example. His pop has stopped drinking and he no longer abuses Paul. Their relationship is on the mend. It'll take a while for Paul to trust him again but they'll get there. Paul's now a confident young man because of you. He'll go places and his dad will be there rooting for him.

"Then there's Jenny. Her mom Gabriella has seen the error of her ways and she now spends quality time with her daughter. You've also broken Jenny free from the influence of the Devil's disciple."

"I'm not too sure about that Isais. Kurt is still hanging around her."

"Sure he is, but it's you he's after and he's using her for bait. He wants to serve you on a plate to his master."

"How do you know all this?"

"I just do."

"Sorry, I'm not accepting that answer Isais, I've taken you into my trust, I think it's time you came clean and I also want to know what's in this for you. Skin-walkers don't normally give up their witchery ways to help God."

Isais suddenly looks very solemn and his eyes fill with tears.

"I'm looking for God to redeem my soul, boy. I want to make reparation for my sins. I want to make up for not saving my son from the Devil."

I know it's been sometime since my word of the day was dumbfounded, but wow, I want to use it now, because I'm totally and utterly dumbfounded.

"What happened to Ashkii?"

"He became one of JoJo's pretty boys. My innocent,

beautiful son became possessed by evil spirits. Just like Kurt, Robbie, and friends."

"But how could you have stopped that?"

"I could have taken him away from here. I could have used my powers for the good and I didn't. I just sat back and let them destroy him. He too, had inherited the powers of his forefathers and JoJo nurtured the evil within him. Allowing evil to take possession of his soul."

"If you could have saved him why didn't you?"

"Because to have powers such as mine, I believed you had to practice evil. My mother was a God fearing woman and she refused to allow her father to develop my supernatural powers that I inherited from him. Therefore I had no idea that I could also do good.

"You asked me previously if I had physically killed anyone. Although I have never murdered, I might as well have been driving the car that Ashkii died in."

"What happened to him?"

"He was driving my car, which he stole. He ran off the road and he burned to death. I can't put it any other way. It's the Navajo belief that when you die, you go to a land that is filled with happiness, has wonderful hunting grounds, and, most importantly, death is not something we should fear. But I know deep down that because he ran with the Devil, he was consumed by the flames meant for the Devil."

Isais puts his head in his hands. I know he is stifling back his tears and I get up from my chair and hug him. He looks at me, tears run down his face, he suddenly looks much younger in years and he continues, "My heart is filled with hope that maybe you are my son, and God has given us a second chance."

"Isais, as much as I would love to be your son, I don't think I am. I've been getting more and more flashbacks recently, which I believe are of my childhood years. Isais,

I see a woman holding me, playing with me, reading to me, the woman I can only assume is my mother. I've seen the pictures that are dotted around your home of your wife and I'm afraid she is not the woman whom I see in my visions."

"I could only hope." Isais looks so sad.

"Look who's morose now."

"Even if you're not my boy, I can at least help you gain your place in heaven. So let's go get them boy."

"Let's go get them." This conversation is sooo heavy. But he's right, I have to prove to God and his elders that I deserve salvation.

§ § §

I am now resolute in helping rid the evil that has now possessed Kurty and those others in our midst that the Red Rider has chosen. I have to do this to show my worthiness and all I have to do now is to hatch a plan.

You're rather quiet. Cat got your tongue? Thinking caps on, come on I need your input. I don't hear those cogs in your head turning yet. Come on. Okay I'll give you until the morning. You go back to sleep, or carry on doing what you were doing. I'm going to spirit over to see Suzie.

§ § §

The hospital corridors are quiet, only the staff on night duty move from room to room, checking on their patients well being. As I pass the nurse's station I cause a slight draft and the paperwork the lead nurse is working on rustles.

Her face bears a puzzled expression as she looks from right to left along the long corridor in search of the origin of the sudden chill she feels.

"Someone must have just walked over my grave." She shivers.

I chuckle, of course she can neither see nor hear me. On seeing nothing untoward she goes back to reading her notes. It can be fun, when I transform into my spiritual state and I cause unexplained happenings. Maybe I do have a devilish streak, I'm just a little scamp at heart, aren't I?

I've entered Suzie's room. *Beep, beep, beep,* that's the sound of her life support paraphernalia. She's lying motionless. I look at her chart; why bother? It's not as if I understand any of the medical jargon. I pray inwardly.

"Hey Suz, my gorgeous girl, it's me, Dan. Come on, wakey, wakey, rise and shine." I kiss her forehead, but she doesn't respond and silence is the reply. "Come on Suzie, I'm missing you in drama class. You were so excited about us both being on stage together. I can't believe you've bailed out on me. We're about to do the kissing scene and I was so looking forward to that with you, it'd be such a laugh. Two good pals having to come over all romantic."

I lay my hands on her forehead. In an attempt to heal her, I exert every piece of mental energy I can to force all the white light from me into her. The problem is, I don't actually know what I'm healing. Angels are supposed to have healing powers and I'm kind of hoping that I just need a bit of practice to develop mine. If I could just get inside her mind, inside her body, maybe I could heal her from the inside out.

I don't know if this is going to work. Maybe I've been spending too much time with a skin-walker, but here I go. God give me the strength to do this, if it is the correct thing to do. The room floods with light, emitting from deep down inside me, from the depths of my soul.

Holy cow, I did it. I've shape shifted into Suzie's body. Wow, this isn't pleasant at all. Every intake of breath is a struggle, paralysis encapsulates her body. Her heart labors to beat.

Oh, Dasher and Blitzen. That has more impact than saying darn it, doesn't it? Oaths, of course, can never leave my lips and they shouldn't leave yours either. I can hear voices coming from the corridor, someone's heading this way. The door opens and in comes the lead nurse, followed closely behind by Jenny.

"I'm surprised you're on your own. It's rather late for a young girl like you to be out and about," says the nurse.

"I was so worried about her, I got my mom to bring me over."

"Okay as long as your parents know where you are."

"Thanks, I won't stay too long."

The nurse leaves the room. Jenny pulls over a chair and sits down. I feel rather awkward about this whole situation, but I'll just have to stay put, what else can I do? Jenny looks so gorgeous, her cheeks are slightly flushed and she has a certain glow about her, but not an angel one.

She takes hold of Suzie's hand and strokes it gently, she leans forward and kisses me, I mean she kisses Suzie. Don't get so excited, it was a peck on the cheek, nothing else. That was sooo good. She sits back in her chair and stares at Suzie.

I don't know if it's my imagination or not, but something strange seems to be happening to Jenny. Strange indeed, OMG her appearance is changing. I'll give you a clue; in the bible it's said that God sent these creatures as a punishment. Someone sent this guy, but it wasn't God. This cannot be happening. I know you should never judge a book by its cover, but this is ridiculous. Unbelievable. I better believe it, because Jenny has transformed into my big locust friend, Loco. Whoa, I think I must be going loco. Astonishment, astonishment.

My Jenny is a demonlet. She's been possessed. This is a real eye opener. Holy cow, talking of eyes, hers are swiveling on their stalks. She's making a throaty sound, it's difficult to hear. I can't say she looks so gorgeous now; in fact she's one ugly dude.

I'm calling her a dude because I could never make disparaging remarks about a lady. In fact, I'm beginning to believe that it's unlikely I'll ever get passed St Peter, the gatekeeper. Those pearly gates may never unlock for me, because I can only think of Jen disparagingly at present.

I have no idea what she plans to do, but I think I'm about to find out. Wow, she's standing up and she's beginning to flap her large wings. OMG the draft she's causing sucks the curtains into the room. The pages of Suzie's medical chart flail, like a sail on a yacht in the midst of a storm. The clip on the board struggles to grip the pages and one of the pages tears in half and floats off to the other side of the room.

"Chiiirp, chiiirp, chiiirp," says Loco deafeningly. She's one noisy old girl.

The room starts to fill with a red vapor. I think I may chuck up the cookies I ate earlier, sometime in the very near future. The stench of rotten eggs is now filling the room. Sorry to be so graphic with the descriptions guys, but this still isn't a scratch and sniff book as far as I know.

She opens her mouth and a large wriggly tongue shoots out of her mouth and is heading towards me. What's with the wriggly, wiggly tongues? No cataglottis for us. You can look the word up later.

If I don't take over Susie's body completely and start moving her limbs, she's going to become Loco food and you know how they like to munch through things. They're worse than me.

Here comes the tongue; no not the sun, but the tongue. Aaagh, missed. I've had to force Suzie's body to the left hand side of the bed. That's confused Loco, how do I know that? By the puzzled look in her swirling eyes. Very attractive I must say. I want to say, look into my swirling pools and call me Ducky.

But no time for frivolity, because she's got over her bewilderment and here she comes. Her big tongue spirals and spits. I slide Suzie's body down the bed, zippo, nah, nah, de nah, nah, she missed. Your aim will need to be better than that.

OMG, she's pulling herself up to her full height, and lunging her full body forward. I raise Suzie's body straight up into the air, she's floating in mid-air vertically. Loco crashes into the bed. I can hear someone approaching and so does Loco, because poof, she's gone. I try to resume Suzie's body in the position she was in before. Hopefully no harm done.

The lead nurse bursts into the room and looks around. I can only assume she's looking for Jenny. She comes over to Suzie's bed and she fiddles about with the knobs on the life support machine. She starts to straighten the bed covers. They are slightly disturbed, but not enough that she would notice that something had gone on here a minute ago. The nurse leans over Suzie and she says, "Where did your friend go to, my dear? It was nice of her to visit anyway, wasn't it?" She lifts the chart from the bottom of the bed, she's noticed that one of the pages has torn. She looks about the floor and spots the missing piece over by the chair. She scratches her head and says, "How on earth did that happen?" She takes another look around and tucks the clipboard under her arm. "Good everything seems to be okay here." If only she knew.

Chapter Thirty-Four

His eyes are like blazing fire, and on his head are many crowns. He has a name written on him that no-one but he himself knows.

Revelation 19:12

What are you doing in here? Can a dude not have any privacy? I was just having a quick shower, minding my own business, and you make an appearance. Just give me a minute and I'll give myself a quick dry with that big fluffy towel over there, if you can hand it to me. So you're too embarrassed to keep your eyes open, I should think so too.

Okay, that's me decent. I've wrapped the towel around my waist, you can open your eyes now. I just need to shave some of this bum fluff off my face, brush my teeth, and I'll be right with you. I rub my hand across the mirror, now I can see what a pretty boy I am. Do you think I need run the clippers over my hair? Yes I agree, I can wait a couple of days.

Holy cow, who's this dude in the mirror? I've never seen him before. I cover my eyes with my hands. Do you think I should have a peek? I know I'm a coward, but I will have to uncover my eyes at some time. I separate my fingers gradually; as I thought, the dude's still looking at me. In fact, everything I do is mirrored. I think I need to have a long hard look at this kid.

I lean forward over the wash-basin. Mmm, he's a good looking kid and there is something familiar about him. He's roundabout my age, my height and weight. There is just that certain something about him that makes me think that I definitely know this dude.

"Hey kid, do I know you?" Scary he's speaking in unison with me. I recognize his voice, I recognize everything about him, I recognize him because he's me. I recognize him, but he's a stranger to me. I know it's me, but what's my name? I'm dumbfounded once again. How about you?

§ § §

"You're very quiet this morning Dan." Aunt Sylvia is making pancakes for my breakfast. I should weigh twenty stone with the amount of food I eat. Angelets must have a good metabolism, is all I can say. She's the best aunt ever and I feel I haven't been as honest with her as I should have been. Although we do have a fantastic relationship, by telling her everything I get up to, I'm scared I will spoil the whole thing we have going on and fail the angel test.

You see; on one hand, I'm scared of being criticized by my peers and on the other, I'm afraid of letting them down. Therefore I hold back in telling her about the things I may be judged on. It's not a good trait, because my peers aren't out to tell me I'm rubbish at everything I do, they just want to help me. They were trainee angels once. They've been there, done that, and bought the t-shirt.

Whilst I know my circumstances are different from other angels, we all have something in common and that's the fact that we can all wear the t-shirt with the logo 'Dead' on it. I think I need to come clean, face my responsibilities.

"Yes, I think there are some things I need to tell you." I have my serious face on.

She turns off the gas hob, wipes her hands over her apron, and sits down beside me.

"I wondered when you would get round to it," she says, smiling.

"I might have known I could have no secrets from you."

"Dan, it's not about keeping secrets, it's about learning and doing the right thing. It's about you being saved."

"I'm not sure where to start."

"How about when you found out that Isais was a skin-walker." She takes hold of my hand, the good news for me is that she is still smiling. I'm dumbfounded, but not totally speechless.

"Okay, it was when ..."

§ § §

Well what was all the panic about? I confessed all, from Loco, Papa B, to having human urges. She took it all in her stride and never once made me feel that she was passing judgment on me.

That's what being a guardian angel is all about, I suppose. She confirmed that the dude in the bathroom must be me getting a glimpse of the real me. If you understand what I'm saying. I had a quick glance in the mirror just a moment ago and I'm back to being Dan Pierce, the mysterious good-looking dude is gone. Hopefully not for too long, though. Not that I'm not handsome as Dan Pierce, of course.

Aunt Sylvia says I'm making good progress, but she still has no confirmation on my true identity. She couldn't confirm as to whether I'm making headway into becoming a fully fledged angel either, because she said it isn't her call. Which is true. I just want it all to come together now, no more waiting, no more wondering.

I'm just being a bit impatient. There you go, you always have to have a little dig at me. At present I don't need any naughty comments from you. Okay that's you told. Friends? Of course we are.

§ § §

I've managed to avoid Jenny most of the day. As luck would have it most of our classes were in different parts of the campus. I came across Kurt on several occasions, but he took no notice of me. Maybe because he has Jenny to do his dirty work now and he can focus on doing other deeds for the Devil.

Enough of my guessing games. I'd better get my thinking cap on, as it's drama class time. Jenny has just walked into the room, and she's all smiles. *Buzzz, buzzz,* yes it's my damn earring; it's decided to come to life once again. Jenny's coming over to me, yes, she's here. I want to puke, but I need to keep my cool and I'll go with the flow.

"Hi Jenny, did you manage to get over to see Suzie last night at any point?" If you could see the grin I have on my face. I should be nominated for an Oscar.

"No, I really had to get my head down and learn these words," says Pinocchio. I meant to say Jenny. I've just noticed what a big nose she has. "Did you?" says Jenny unashamedly. Pass me the barf bag. I can tell you this girl is as cool as a cucumber.

"Yes, for a little while, just before dinner." Okay, I could be Pinocchio's triplet brother.

"Everyone in the hair salon scene, please take your places. Dan and Jenny, that includes you, if you can spare the time." We're interrupted by Miss Summerville who's sounding a little on the grumpy side today. I hope I'm not on the receiving end of her wrath. Jenny, I, and the other performers take our positions on stage. Cath, aka Jenny, is supposed to be having her hair done.

Louise is playing the hairdresser and she starts to pin up Jenny's hair. Freddy, aka me, is hanging around waiting on his amour. I'm acting rather lost and forlorn, as most males do when they're in the vicinity of a lady's hair salon. Louise finishes her attempt at 'haute coiffeuse' and Jenny gets up from where she's sitting in front of a make shift mirror. Walking towards me, she says, "Oh darling, I hope you haven't been too bored, waiting for me."

"Madam, your husband was not bored. He has been admiring you from afar," says Louise.

"Have you darling, have you?" says Jenny lovingly.

"Yes I have, you look so beautiful," I say. I can tell, you're impressed. Not a stutter or a stammer utters from my lips. Or even a retch, as I spout these words of love to her. I'm a real cool dude, in fact I'm so cool towards her, I probably should be called a cold fish.

Although she hasn't transformed into Loco, she might as well have, as far as I'm concerned. My feelings for her have vanished, just as she did from Suzie's room last night.

"Dan, I need more enthusiasm from you. Don't be such a cold fish. You're in love with her," shouts Miss Summerville.

Jenny and I move across the stage hand in hand, she has a real tight grip of me. We stop center stage and I take her into my arms. She looks into my eyes, I can feel her pale blue eyes burn into my soul. The devil has definitely possessed hers, that's for sure.

Wow, can you hear that noise? That's the cogs in my brain turning around, *clink, clink, clink.* I need to focus, to do what I need to do now. If I pull this one off, I'll be real impressed and so will you. As she pushes her slim body into mine, my eyes turn a fiery red and her body suddenly goes limp.

"Whoa, Miss Summerville, Jenny seems to have fainted." Reeesult.

Chapter Thirty-Five

I looked, and there before me was a white horse! Its rider held a bow, and he was given a crown, and he rode out as a conqueror bent on conquest.

Revelation 6:2

Mmm, mmm, corn bread, deep fried chicken, and peppers stuffed with fried beans, with coconut custard to follow. I bet you wish this was a scratch and taste book. After I've eaten the beans, I'll be butt burping all night. Sorry, I'm a wee bit vulgar, but it's all in the sake of having fun.

After my hectic day it's great to be sitting down for dinner. Isais is going to take me over to the hospital later. Paul's already over there with his dad. You know George has really sorted himself out. The man had been finding it really hard to cope with the death of Paul's mom. But after some counseling and a few long chats with Aunt Sylvia, he's coming together just fine.

When I looked in the mirror before I came through for dinner, I had a visit from that real handsome dude, but I'm still no nearer to recalling any of his details. He left as quick as he appeared, but I'm hoping that we'll both become a bit more familiar in the near future.

"Is that okay for you, Dan?" Aunt Sylvia joins me at the table. I nod, as my mouth is full of beans and well it's rude to talk with your mouth full. I lift a piece of corn bread and bite on it, I chew it rapidly and swallow. I lay down the remainder of the slice, the indents of my teeth can still be seen on the thick butter that it's spread with. Mmm, what to munch next. I lift a breaded chicken drumstick and I open my mouth to take a bite and whoa, purple lion faces and locusts fill my head. I drop my chicken and stand up abruptly.

"You must go, Dan, Paul and Suzie are in danger," says Aunt Sylvia.

I leave my human shell immediately and I go through the front-door. Awesome, a huge ghostly, white stallion rears on its hind legs and neighs loudly. Isais has done his shape-shifting thing again.

I climb onto his back, which is covered by a vibrant colored saddle blanket. I grip onto his long white mane and we take to the air. I'm not sure how we're actually flying because he doesn't have wings like Pegasus. But I'm rubbish at physics anyway, so even if I knew, I would never be able to explain it to you.

We reach the hospital in neigh time, it sounds better if you say it with a Scots accent. My white horse bursts through the window of Suzie's room. Paul is lying unconscious on the floor and a purple faced Kurt is standing over him. Whoa, the rasping noises he's making are deafening. His pincers are clicking in anticipation of snipping Paul's life away.

Loco is chirping at the top of her voice, they seem to be oblivious of our arrival. They're communicating excitedly with each other. But there's no time to translate, so trust me when I say the word death features prominently in their dialogue. Loco's standing on her back legs and she's biting at the wiring of the machines that are keeping Suzie in this world.

I jump onto her back, her eyes rotate and, using her antennae to tug at me, she attempts to pull me off of her. I'm forcing her wings closed with the strength of my knees. It's difficult for me to keep onboard, but I'm gripping onto her long golden locks with all my might. I wonder what shampoo she uses, because her hair is in fantastic condition.

As she spins around in an effort to throw me, I see

my trusty steed kick purple boy to the ground with his silver hooves. I'd love to applaud him, but I have other pressing matters to be getting on with. One such pressing matter is Loco's shell. It's so solid that it's stopping me from forcing white light through her body.

I'm going to have to find a chink in her armor. I place my hands over her eyes and she shrieks. She bucks like a rodeo pony, but I've managed to hook into the little grooves on her wings. She swings her head around and she's thumped me so hard that I fly across the room. *Thump,* that was me hitting the floor hard.

I'm up on my feet, but I need to catch my breath. I look over towards my white horse; he seems to have everything under control. Each time purple dude tries to get up, the big guy rears up and kicks him to the floor. But no rest for the wicked, here she blows. Loco's flying towards me, her wings whirr. They're whirring so fast I can hardly see them.

She's backed me into a corner, no place to go, no place to hide. If what I'm about to do now fails, you can only guess how the story is going to end. Say a prayer, because I'm now living on one.

"It doesn't need to be like this Jenny." She doesn't respond to me. "Do you hear what I'm saying Jen? It doesn't need to be this way. We can be together, for always."

She's hovering over me, her jaws are open. I'm about to be chewed like a piece of gum and she'll blow me out in bubbles. I close my eyes in anticipation and I put my head on my knees. I'm not looking forward to being swallowed by a locust.

Duh, nothing's happened. I open my eyes and Loco is turning back into Jen. It's the strangest sight, Jenny's face is smiling at me, but her body is still that of a large bug.

"I knew you wouldn't choose God over me. You love

me. We must destroy them all, then we can be together for always. Just like Catherine and Frederic." She's sitting on the floor beside me, her transformation is complete. She's so beautiful, so beautiful that I want to kiss her, yes you heard correct. I lean forward, she leans forward, I can smell her sweet perfume. Our lips are a fraction of an inch apart. Zzz, zzz, zzz, that noise is the electrical force between us.

Zzzzzp, zzzzzp, that's the white light leaving me and penetrating into her body. She judders, her body shatters into pieces, like broken glass. The bits break up into smaller pieces, then again, finally turning into dust. Wind fills the room and Jenny's gone, sucked through the window into the Arizona sky.

"Sorry Jenny, you should have read the ending of the play. Cath and Freddie aren't together for always. Cath dies." I knew I would find a chink in her armor. Me being her vulnerable spot. I knew she had strong feelings for me, but I was too late to save her. She had played with fire too long. If I had kissed her, her evil powers would have possessed me. It was a good thing I didn't give in to temptation; it would have been the kiss of death for me.

Talking of fire, my reliable horse is about to end the purple monster's reign of terror. He opens his great mouth and his shiny silver teeth bite into the softer underbelly of his opposition. *Crrrunch,* that was the teeth piercing through Kurty's shell. Just like the others, the purple monster starts to degenerate.

Firstly his body explodes into tiny fragments, then into a fine powder, then he's gone, gone into the night. I'm sure they won't feel out of place in the desert, not so far from here.

Chapter Thirty-Six

Like a dream he flies away, no more to be found, banished like a vision of the night. The eye that saw him will not see him again; his place will look on him no more.

Job 20:8.9

"Come on in Isais," says Aunt Sylvia. Isais enters the kitchen sheepishly. He resembles some kid that's been up to mischief. "Sit down beside Dan, he has a few things he wants to tell you before he goes." Aunt Sylvia sure isn't showing any kind of indifference towards Isais.

There's definitely nothing private around here. You better listen too, because what I have to say will affect you as well. Isais sits down opposite me, wow, does he look gloomy. I clear my throat.

"I thought you should know that when tomorrow dawns, I'll be gone," I say. Isais opens his mouth to speak, but I raise my finger to my lips to hush him momentarily. I need to say what I've got to say without interruptions. So be warned, hush now. "The elders have told me my work is finished here. Although they've made it clear I'm not on the home stretch yet, I still have more to do.

"I made mistakes along the way and hopefully I can learn from them. Then one day, all going well, I'll be allowed to shake hands with Saint Peter on my way in through the pearly gates."

"I'll be sorry to see you go boy. I told you before how I wished you were my son."

"Thanks Isais, you'll make me blush. But I do have some news for you on that front. I've been given permission from the elders to disclose this information to you. Your son made massive mistakes in his life and he did a lot of bad things, as you already know. But what you don't know is, that the night he was killed, he stole your car to try and get away from the situation he had become embroiled in.

"He had told Kurt that he wanted out, he didn't want to continue with his evil ways. Ashkii was full of remorse for all the things he had done. But the Devil wasn't letting go of one of his promising trainees, no siree.

"Kurt was ordered to destroy him, so that night he followed him, with Robbie and Jenny along for the ride. Kurt managed to force him off the road and the rest you know. With JoJo's help they made sure that any evidence that would have shown involvement of another vehicle was destroyed."

"Has God accepted my boy into his fold?"

"No, not quite. All I can say for now, his soul has been spared. He's being held in a place of purification. It's kind of like a rehab clinic for sinners. The support you have given me has helped his cause and yours. He'll be okay."

"Thank you Dan, I'll miss you boy. Come and give me a big hug. I promise I won't hug you too tight." Isais is already up on his feet with his arms open. I hug him and give his cheek a massive kiss. It seems I made the right decision in putting my faith and trust in him. But oh boy, it could have all went wrong.

"I'll miss you too. I hope that maybe someday we'll meet again. If you don't mind Isais, I've got a few other things to take care of. So I'll leave you to have some of Aunt Sylvia's pie." I hug him again.

"Sure boy, you go and do what you have to do." Tears run down his face as he watches me leave the room.

§ § §

"More, more, more." The crowd roar and applaud

enthusiastically as Paul and Suzie step forward to take a bow. They make a much better Cath and Freddy than Jenny and I ever did. As the crowd give them an ovation, Paul takes Suzie into his arms and OMG, what a smacker. I never knew the boy had it in him. Go big boy, go. The kiss lingers for some time and the delighted audience cheers.

From where I'm lurking in the shadows of the school theater, I can have a good look around. The first pair I spot are Paul's pop and gran. They look so proud. Oh, and there's Suzie's parents, clapping and cheering like mad.

Poor Suzie, she's been through the mill. But hey, ho, things have all been put right and nobody knows any better. Not even her mom will have any recollection of what's gone on here. But that woman is real spooky.

I received an email a couple of minutes ago. Ashkii's soul has now been cleansed, so he's not going to be joining his friends Kurt, Robbie, and Jenny's souls in the great abyss. I should explain that their demise actually happened some time ago, they were in the car behind Ashkii's and it ran off the road too.

Okay, you don't believe that statement because my coming here wasn't until after Ashkii died. But as I explained when I first arrived, time doesn't pass the same way as it does on Earth in the spirit world. I'll leave you with the thought that maybe time doesn't really happen the way you perceive it on Earth either. Maybe time can be reversed and some things can be changed, not all, but some. It's a conundrum isn't it?

That's it; Wingate's world has been returned to normality. Guardian angels, like Aunt Sylvia, will stand guard and send out an SOS if all hell breaks out again.

§ § §

Well kiddo, it's just you and me against the world.

Hope you've enjoyed our little adventure. I know we've had some hairy, scary times. But I never told you it was going to be otherwise, did I? No.

I'm beat, let's go to bed. What are you doing? I didn't mean for us to go to bed together, I meant, I'll see you in the morning. It's not a slumber party you know. I'm glad we cleared that little misunderstanding up. Phew, okay, moving on; goodnight, God bless, and when we meet up in the morning, we'll take it from there. Night, night, don't let the bugs bite. Oh, I wish I could give you a big hug. I love hugs.

§ § §

Thank goodness you decided to join me. Satan is still at large, so the hunt goes on. I'm on my way to a place called Tuktoyakluk. It seems the locals call it Tuk and if it's good enough for them, it's good enough for me. Now I need to tell you about my new amigo, his name is…

About the Author

Christina Rowell worked in banking and finance for more years than she cares to remember, but is now a full time author and a member of The Society of Authors. She lives with her husband in Scotland. Salvation No Kissing Required is her debut novel. She's at present working on the sequel. Her official blog can be found http://devilslayingamongstotherthings.blogspot.co.uk

Trademarks Acknowledgment

The author acknowledges the trademark status and trademark owners of the following wordmarks mentioned in this work of fiction:

Nissan: Nissan Motor Company Ltd

Pontiac GTO: General Motors

Plymouth Road Runner: Chrysler Group LLC.

Deuce coupe: Ford Motor Company

Goggle (called Goddle in ms): Google Inc.

Wikipedia (called Godipedia in ms): Wikimedia Foundation, Inc.

1999 Ford Cobra: Ford Motor Company

A Farewell to Arms (play): Simon & Schuster Inc.

CPSIA information can be obtained at www.ICGtesting.com
Printed in the USA
LVOW131341280613

340697LV00001B/58/P